# THE PLEASURE DOME

## THE SCIENCE OFFICER: VOLUME 4

### BLAZE WARD

KRP

**The Pleasure Dome**
**Volume 4**
Blaze Ward
Copyright © 2017 Blaze Ward
All rights reserved
Published by Knotted Road Press
www.KnottedRoadPress.com

ISBN: 978-1-943663-44-6


Cover art:
Copyright © Sdecoret | Dreamstime.com - Sunrise Over Planets In Space Photo
Copyright © Ambassador806 | Dreamstime.com - Spartan Warrior Helmet Photo

*Xanadu* is a quote from *Kubla Khan* by Samuel Taylor Coleridge



**Reviews**
It's true. Reviews help me sell more books. If you've enjoyed this story, please consider leaving a review of it on your favorite site.

**Never miss a release!**
If you'd like to be notified of new releases, sign up for my newsletter.

I will never spam you or use your email for nefarious purposes. You can also unsubscribe at any time.

http://www.blazeward.com/newsletter/

# ALSO BY BLAZE WARD

## Star Tribes

*WinterStar*

*SeekerStar*

*SeptStar*

*SwiftStar*

*MorningStar*

## The Handsome Rob Gigs

*Can't Shoot Straight Gang*

*Can't Shoot Straight Gang Returns*

*Hunting Handsome Rob*

## The Jessica Keller Chronicles

*Auberon*

*Queen of the Pirates*

*Last of the Immortals*

*Goddess of War*

*Flight of the Blackbird*

*The Red Admiral*

*St. Legier*

*Winterhome*

*Petron*

## CS-405

*Queen Anne's Revenge*

*Call of the Star Dragon*

*Shadow of the Star Dragon*

*Trial of the Star Dragon*

# BOOK NINE: MERCENARY

PART ONE

JAVIER HAD NEVER BEEN one for gear lust.

It had never been about fast cars or fancy starships, with the sole exception of Suvi and *Mielikki*. The rest of the time, whatever was necessary to get him to the next gig, the next station, the next bar was enough.

But that was before he laid eyes on the Land Leviathan.

Starships were cool and all. As were AI systems smart enough to compose music and poetry.

Hell, he even knew one like that.

But the Land Leviathan marked that point where you were truly living in a galaxy wealthy beyond ancient dreams of avarice, regardless of what anyone else thought on the topic. For the longest moment, he considered how he would go about stealing it.

"Why are we here, again?" Javier finally asked Zakhar Sokolov, seated next to him in the backseat of the VTOL limo as they slowly descended on the giant metal train from above, a tiny eagle chasing a monstrous snake across a salmon-colored desert wasteland.

Ten square cars, each sixty meters on a side and at least

half that tall. Connected like a train, except rumbling slowly across the sand and rock on treads at least four meters tall instead of rails. From where Javier sat, it looked vaguely like an ocean liner, with the top of each of the ten sections dedicated to a different task, including a landing deck, a swimming pool, an amphitheater, and something that looked suspiciously like a barbeque pit big enough for a whole pig.

Stealing it would be difficult. He could see a big, honking gun turret up front, and two smaller, flanking ones at the rear, plus six air-defense cannons on the sides. The last car had a semi-open bay at ground level, containing a variety of ground and skimmer combat vehicles, including at least two that looked remarkably like main battle tanks from one of Suvi's favorite video games.

Clearly, someone had let their paranoia get the better of them. Or seriously considered the sort of gear lust that this level of cash expenditure would engender in someone like Javier Aritza.

And this wasn't a rolling resort, even if it looked like one.

No, this was somebody's personal land yacht. Complete with a crew and staff of three to five hundred. One of the most expensive vehicles ever manufactured on the surface of any planet.

Chicken feed.

The man seated beside Javier stirred. He might have been napping. All the more reason to wake him up.

"Because someone wanted to hire a bad-ass mercenary named Navarre," the man replied, stretching. "And she seems to think I'm one of the few people in the galaxy able to locate the man."

Javier nodded. It was true. He was.

Zakhar Sokolov. Captain of the private service strike corvette, *Storm Gauntlet*, a vessel meandering back and forth across legality as situations demanded.

Average, if you met him on the street. 1.8 meters tall. Ordinary build. Shaved head with a salt and pepper Van Dyke. Mid-fifties lines on his face. Nothing interesting at all.

At least until he turned on that *Captain thing*. Then he was all charm and bad-ass.

Javier had never gotten the hang of being a command officer. Liking people was probably a requirement.

A bridge too far.

"That explains why I'm here, Zakhar," Javier volleyed the conversation back across the tiny enclosed space. "Not you."

Javier watched the man who was technically his superior officer, possibly his owner, depending on how you wanted to slice things, chew on his next sentence, like a cow with good cud.

Whatever lies were coming must be pretty amazing.

Since Javier, posing as Navarre, had rescued his own mortal enemy, Djamila Sykora, Zakhar Sokolov's *Dragoon*, at *Meehu Platform*, Javier's relationship with Sokolov and the rest of the crew had changed. It had really started at *A'Nacia*, when he saved all their butts from the killer-robot mine field, and then rescued Wilhelmina Teague from eternity, before he made the rest of them rather wealthy.

The crew no longer really considered him a slave they had captured. Even an honored one like a modern Janissary. No, these days he was just another officer in charge, just another Centurion.

The Science Officer. And all that implied.

Those folks he generally liked well enough to let them out of his revenge.

But he hadn't paid off his debt bond to Sokolov. And he still hadn't killed Sykora.

"That comes after we meet with the contact," Captain Sokolov said simply. "You and I are going to need to have a conversation. Without the rest of the crew around."

Javier bit back the sarcastic riposte poised on the tip of his tongue. The last one of *those* conversations had sent him to rescuing Sykora from her captor, when he could have easily fled across deep space and made it home and left the woman to her well-deserved fate. And he could have taken Suvi with him, still tucked quietly into her handheld scout probe, even if now it was the size of a soccer ball.

He hadn't, because he had given his word as an officer and a gentleman of Bryce, according to the statement on the commissioning papers each man had received upon graduating the Academy and becoming officers of the Concord Navy, once upon a long time ago. Literally, his ransom, to use the archaic term.

Going back on that, even with people like this, would make Javier the one thing he despised most in the galaxy.

A pirate.

*One of those conversations, Zakhar?*

Javier held his tongue, and his peace. They were on the final approach to the last car of the Land Leviathan.

Soon enough, he would know the truth.

Hopefully, he wouldn't have to kill as many people this time.

Unless they were pirates.

---

JAVIER REALLY DIDN'T WANT to go anywhere as *Navarre*, even in his own mind, but the situation demanded it. Someone wanted to hire the psycho who had killed Abraam Tamaz and his entire crew of the Q-freighter *Salekhard*. Singlehandedly.

This wasn't going to be a tea and crumpets kind of meeting.

If he didn't owe Zakhar Sokolov so much money, he might have refused. Zakhar might have even let it go.

But there was a lot of potential money on the table. Maybe enough to get his freedom and buy his botany station back in the deal.

No chicken should have to spend one day more than necessary with pirates. Even nice ones like *Storm Gauntlet*.

They landed with the soft blush that told Javier most passengers boarding like this were screamers when something happened they found unwelcome.

Up close, the Land Leviathan made all of Javier's dreams of avarice suddenly junior varsity. It got worse as his eyes progressed from place to place.

Entire walkways, everywhere he looked, appeared to be plated over with gold. Granted, most younger solar systems had enough of the material that it had almost no value in and of itself except as decoration, but people still used it as a measure of wealth. Of Power.

Of the ability to just have tons of the stuff as ornament. Simply because it was gold.

They were met at the landing by a hard man in a well-tailored suit, and two killers in loose, black outfits. Javier knew the type. One dressed up to impress you with his culture. Two more to kill you if you got out of line.

Hard people. It was a hard business.

*Navarre* came to the fore as Javier handed the man in the suit his smaller belt, with the holster for a pulse pistol and a fighting poniard. This wasn't that kind of meeting. He hoped.

He settled for walking in the man's wake, Sokolov trailing, with the two others behind that.

The desert planet was hot, so he had cut down what he thought of as the Navarre costume.

Twenty-ring lace up boots in glossy neo-leather, with

curb-stomping soles and hull-metal toes. Bright red laces all the way up and double-knotted at the top.

Knee-length britches out of dark maroon corduroy, with heavy leather combat padding along the outer edge in case someone out of a Chop-sockey movie kicked him. The socks were much lighter fabric today, and only as tall as the boots, rather than covering the knees.

Sixteen-centimeter-tall leather belt around his middle, with a canary-yellow sash tied around that.

Up top, the sleeveless doublet in that same maroon corduroy as the britches, but with two rows of buttons that ran from the inside of his hips to the middle of his collar-bones.

He had skipped the white shirt he would normally wear underneath and left the top part of the doublet unbuttoned, showing off muscles and hairy bits. Time well spent in the gym over the last six months.

And just for the hell of it, Javier had kept the cloth tied around his forehead, with a *Neu Berne* Assault Marine logo in the middle.

It was a look. It had even worked to convince people that he was a sadistic killer.

Killing a lot of people at *Meehu Platform* had helped.

But those people had been pirates. They'd had it coming.

The long walk finally ended somewhere around the third car back from the prow. Javier had lost track of the number of times they had exited a section into heat, crossed a catwalk, and entered the next. He probably should have been paying closer attention, but Navarre was an unwelcome guest in his head.

If only there was some other way to do this, without pretending to be *him*.

The last surprise today was probably the least surprising,

if he'd have given it more thought and less brooding. There weren't that many people who even knew about Navarre.

And there she was.

The only time they had met had been on *Meehu Platform*, when Javier as Navarre was busy getting close enough to Tamaz to rescue Sykora.

Stewart Lace.

Javier had looked up her name later, after Tamaz was dead, to make sure he wouldn't have a problem with her.

She was still dressed like a banker and still in good shape, if thickening with age. Mid-fifties, perhaps, from the lines about her, so around Zakhar's age, and a decade older than Javier. A little more solid than he liked them, but still very well-kept.

Her beauty had that slowly-aging thing going, coming down from an amazing starting point, like the best wines, even as she wore little makeup and kept her hair buzzed to perhaps three or four millimeters long.

Her eyes were what did it. They had the intelligence of an alpha predator, even as they smiled rather warmly at him.

Javier wondered if she had started out as a lawyer or a prostitute forty years ago, and how she had managed to retain some level of humanity for this long. She wasn't really his type, Javier liked his women skinnier, but she was probably one of the few he had ever met who could have a good conversation over breakfast, afterwards.

He doubted that was why she had brought him here.

She rose as they entered the cozy little salon, done up in soft pastel fabrics and paint. Peach. Aqua. Seafoam.

Silk sofas and antique wooden side tables. Money.

"Captain Sokolov," Lace said as she shook his hand. "Captain Navarre. I'm surprised you didn't bring your dangerous sidekick."

"She's guarding the ship," Javier said with a noncommittal growl.

Technically, the woman was referring to 'Mina, but she was hopefully gone away and safe. Converting the galaxy up from being heathens into civilized folk. Sykora could probably be convinced to sub for her, in a pinch. Especially if she got to beat people up.

Djamila Sykora lived for that.

"I see," Lace said. "Please, join me."

Javier had to suppress an inappropriate giggle. The room had been set for tea and cucumber sandwiches.

Seriously. Antique, bone china. Small plates with cucumber and dill-cream triangles of bread.

All those classes in deportment, back at Bryce Academy, all that preparation to be here now as *Navarre*, and here he was.

Both he and Sokolov managed to drink with pinkies out. Concord Fleet Officers, and all that.

Javier could see the woman smile knowingly as she watched them.

*So, surprised you got someone with more manners than Abraam Tamaz, lady? Two of them?*

The only thing he got out of the small talk was that she didn't own the Land Leviathan, but was representing the iron snake's owner in this deal. So stealing it was probably right out. And buying it outright would take the annual budget of some medium-sized planets.

Javier made a note to check his investment portfolio sometime. Most of it had been cut to pieces when Sokolov's crew had dismembered Suvi. The rest was hidden in civilized places where Sokolov's pirates wouldn't let him go without adult supervision. And he had no intention of letting that bunch of yahoos anywhere near his bank account.

That could wait until he got free and had to start over.

"I've been doing some research," Madame Lace said finally, placing her teacup just so and leaning back with a vague smile. "Captain Navarre didn't seem to exist before the incident on *Meehu Platform*. And seems to have disappeared afterwards."

Javier felt Sokolov tense, ever so slightly.

He was personally neither here nor there.

The moment stretched.

"And?" Javier finally said.

Her smile turned a few degrees warmer. Not actually warm, but less predatory.

It was just the three of them, with hard-man and his two killers somewhere outside.

Either she trusted her defensive systems, or didn't think violence would come up in the conversation.

"And so that entire operation appears to have been an elaborate con job," she said. "Designed to get someone close enough to Captain Tamaz to rescue a hostage, escape safely, and lead him to his death."

She paused, in case one of the men wanted to speak, but Sokolov had clammed up.

"Close enough," Javier finally demurred. "I would have phrased it: *…and kill him like a rabid dog.*"

"I see."

More pause.

"The galaxy is a better place without people like Abraam Tamaz," Javier finally offered.

"Indeed, one could make that case," Lace said, her eyes boring in on Javier. "And if I hadn't been there at the time, Captain Navarre would have probably disappeared from all human cognition, wouldn't he?"

Javier just sat and watched her for a few moments. Navarre would have said something cold and biting into the gap. Wanted to. Was at the tip of his mind, offering the words.

Certainly, that would be one path forward.

Just turn into Navarre full-time until he paid off his debt to Sokolov and got his life back. It would make things simpler. Cleaner.

And it would take him back to where he was before. Years ago. Put that blackness back in the center of his soul, instead of stuffed into a locked closet, where it belonged. Remind him why he had two ex-wives.

*Not for you to unlock, lady. Not for any of you.*

"So," Javier ventured, shoving Navarre to one side. "Did you need princesses rescued or dragons slain?"

Navarre was still more of a *Kill the princess, rape the troll, burn the treasure* sort of person, anyway.

Stewart Lace studied Javier closely. More closely.

Like she could see the two men at war inside his head.

She smiled with just the right level of empathy. Neither of his wives had ever managed that.

"A little of both, actually," she finally replied.

Javier felt an eyebrow ascend of its own volition.

"There exists a box," Lace continued, holding up her hands to encompass a space just large enough to store a pair of tiny stiletto heels with frilly puffs on the front. "Through a complicated chain of conversations, my principal has been asked to see to the destruction of the contents of that box. They will pay well. There is an even greater bounty if the contents can be recovered instead."

Javier leaned back and scowled. Navarre was close to saying *I told you so* in his head.

Anyone wanting Navarre wasn't going to be particular about collateral damage. That man had a reputation, at least with the bystanders.

There hadn't been any survivors.

"How much?" Javier asked, cutting to the chase to see how serious these people were.

The number she quoted as an *opening bid* nearly made Javier drop his tea cup. He could suddenly see why Sokolov was here.

That man had a vested interest in making sure the money passed through his hands first.

Javier's cut would still get him within spitting distance of buying his freedom. Another year, or another score like that, and he could probably buy back his chickens and his botany station outright, as well.

Outwardly, Javier nodded calmly. Opening bid. Still several rounds before they got to the final hole card and the serious money.

"Where is it?" he asked.

That much money could only come from someone with planetary wealth at their command. The sort of people who could build a Land Leviathan and occasionally pack it up and take it to a new planet when this one got boring. People who owned whole planets, whole systems, in fee simple.

Dangerous people. Usually quite vicious because nobody has ever been allowed to tell them *No* in their entire lives.

"*Shangdu*," she replied with a biting smile.

"I'm not familiar with that planet," Zakhar spoke up suddenly, in an earnest voice out of place with the man's normally growliness.

"It isn't a planet, Sokolov," Navarre replied, spitting the words out like a grain mill. "It's a starship.

At Xanadu did Kublai Khan

A stately pleasure dome decree…

*Shangdu* is the correct Chinese place name."

"I see," Zakhar replied icily, giving Javier a dose of stinkeye for quoting ancient poetry at him in public.

Javier, in turn, gave Lace a dose of the stinkeye.

"Even bigger reward for recovering it?" he asked.

"Indeed," she agreed. "And I can get you the introductions to get you aboard, depending on your plan. Thoughts?"

"I would like to spend a day or so aboard the Land Leviathan," Javier replied. "Let us have dinner, and spend more time hammering out details. We can come to some consensus tomorrow."

"Excellent," she said, rising. "I will get you situated, and we will convene for dinner in about five hours, gentlemen."

Javier rose, and followed Sokolov out and through the nicer parts of the vessel.

Someone wanted to hire Navarre. Someone probably expecting a mass casualty incident that they could disavow later.

That would be rude. Doubly so on one of the modern age's largest starships, a private playground for the wealthiest elites.

A great way to make a galaxy full of blood enemies.

Javier couldn't do that. Navarre couldn't make him.

But still, he was looking forward to visiting *The Pleasure Dome*.

Again.

PART TWO

ZAKHAR WAITED until he and Javier were nominally alone. The conversation could probably be recorded or transmitted, if that lady banker cared enough. Zakhar had no intention of discussing anything truly incriminating in a place like this.

He was already here hat in hand. No reason to give her or them anything more with which to blackmail him.

This salon was part of a private suite. Two bedrooms off of a central area that was somewhere between hunting lodge and salon. Comfortable, expensive furnishings just masculine enough to make it look tough, but just feminine enough to make it intellectual, rather than barbaric.

Zakhar watched Aritza walk to the bar along one wall, pour a finger of something, and slug it back in a single, hard motion. He would have to wait to see if the alcohol helped or hindered.

Instead, Zakhar pulled up a comfortable-looking leather chair and settled himself into it. Less confrontational, he hoped.

"I got most of the story from Shepherd Teague, before

she left," Zakhar said, drawing Javier's eyes and then his whole body around.

Javier's look was non-committal.

"I doubt it."

He poured another finger of something, but held it this time, looking like a prop.

"I have concerns about this proposed operation," Zakhar concluded.

Aritza looked angry. But he also looked human, which was good. According to Wilhelmina Teague, Navarre had turned the man into a monster from the cold, empty darkness.

"Such as?" Javier finally drawled sarcastically before finishing the second shot and pouring another.

"She specifically asked for Navarre," Zakhar replied. "Based on what he did at *Meehu Platform*."

Javier just eyed him, so Zakhar plowed ahead.

"That's not the sort of reputation I desire," Zakhar continued. "That's not the sort of person I wish to be known as."

"You're a pirate, Sokolov," Javier snarled without ever raising his voice. "And a slaver. I don't think you've got a lot of ground to stand on, here."

Zakhar stopped himself from jumping up to confront the man. This was why he had sat before he spoke.

"I've done indefensible things, mister," Zakhar agreed. "I'll grant you that. But doing to *Shangdu* what you did to Tamaz is not something I will allow."

"It would be worth a tremendous amount of money, Sokolov," his Science Officer, his *slave*, fired back angrily. "Enough that you'll be that much closer to being done with me."

"I don't care, Javier."

"Well I do," the man growled, stopping to slug back the

next finger of whiskey in the glass. "It's that much closer to me being free."

Zakhar watched Javier pour another.

"Anything to get away?" Zakhar asked.

"Damned straight," Javier replied.

"You could have escaped, Javier," Zakhar countered. "More than once."

"You don't get to win, Zakhar."

That shot vanished into Javier's mouth.

He watched Javier pour another finger into the glass, two, heavier this time. He hammered it back in a single, ugly gulp and fixed angry eyes on Zakhar.

"You have my ransom, Sokolov, my word of honor as a gentleman," Javier continued in a nasty, vicious voice. "You will get your money. And there is nothing you can do to stop me. If this deal is too much for your squeamish stomach to handle, then you and I are going to have a problem."

"Javier, it is evil," Zakhar said, nearly pled. "Nothing more. Nothing less. If you feel that strongly, I'm willing to walk away right now, and credit what would have been your share of the deal against your debt. I will not do evil."

An offer like that, and Javier didn't even blink.

"You don't even know what evil is, Sokolov," Aritza sneered at him.

That brought Zakhar out of his chair.

"Oh, no, Aritza. I understand evil," Zakhar snarled quietly as the two men were nearly nose to nose. "I've *been* evil."

Javier stared at him for a moment, and then laughed.

The son of a bitch laughed.

Zakhar stood there, rigid with rage, not trusting himself to keep from strangling his Science Officer. Or punching him.

Javier smiled, turned back to the bar, and grabbed a second highball glass, pouring a shot of whiskey in.

"Good," Javier said with a canary-eating grin as he handed Zakhar the glass and tapped the two together. "Because we're going to do this my way, and see if we can pull off the caper of the century without a single person getting hurt."

"And Navarre?" Zakhar asked, suddenly finding himself on squishy ground.

"Navarre was appropriate to dealing with Tamaz and *Salekhard*, Zakhar," Javier said. "On *Shangdu*, most of them will be children with a lot of money but not the sense God gave a goose."

"And the rest?" Zakhar asked.

"She might be the most dangerous person in the galaxy."

*She?*

# PART THREE

AT LEAST, Javier thought to himself, watching his assistant/minder/bodyguard, Ilan had turned into a pretty competent Machinist's Mate. And the man could keep the chickens fed and safe for a week, and the botany station from catching fire, while Javier had been down on the planet.

Ilan sat across from him now, happily munching a *sandwich*, of some sort.

"So why did it take four days to do your deal, sir?" Ilan asked around a bite.

Javier considered the *casserole* on the plate before him. Industrial cheese. Previously-frozen vegetables of uncertain ancestry. Meat-like substance.

At least the rotini noodles tasted right. It was really hard to screw up rotini. Not that he felt like challenging the cooks around here, or anything.

Javier contemplated his fork like a man considering seppuku. Which wasn't fair to the wardroom cooks. They were just working on a much smaller budget than Stewart Lace.

He sniffed at the casserole anyway.

"Sir?" Ilan hesitated.

"Could have been done in two, Ilan," Javier sighed. "But they had real, fresh cream."

"How fresh?"

Ilan put his sandwich down and grabbed his glass of *something* to drink. Not a good vintage of wine, nor an exquisite Scotch-style whiskey.

"They keep four cows in a small petting zoo, Ilan," Javier said.

Even a man who kept chickens in deep space could be awed at the cost and effort to keep cows.

"You mean, like, real ones?"

Ilan's eyes got big. And this was the man tasked with making sure all of Javier's fruit trees and vegetable gardens got watered regularly when he was off having adventures.

Javier enjoyed being bribed with top notch food to consider doing a job he had already accepted in his head in the first five minutes.

"Yeah," Javier agreed. "Real ones."

Ilan started to say something, changed his mind, and fell uncharacteristically silent.

Javier watched him grab his plate and glass, stand up, and vanish as if his ass was on fire.

Weren't many people could do that to Ilan.

Javier waited.

Sure enough, someone had silently planted an oak tree on the deck behind him. That made it even fewer.

As tall as he was in the torso, Javier was still only looking at her belt buckle when he turned to glance behind him. *Storm Gauntlet's Dragoon*, her master of close combat.

Djamila Sykora.

The Ballerina of Death.

Javier let his eyes roam northward as she stood there.

It had been a year since they had met, the first time she had shot him.

Two point one meters of woman, built like a rugby player with muscles in places Javier wasn't even sure he had places, and he was in better shape than most of this crew.

Dressed today in black slacks, maroon shirt, and a black tunic. Black combat boots with a polish clean enough that Javier could have used them to shave with.

Powerful thighs, reasonable waist, V-shaped torso with small breasts atop big pecs.

The bones in her face were female. Not particularly delicate. Definitely not feminine.

Brown hair worn short to fit inside an armoured lifesuit, buzzed very short on the sides and spiked into a petite Mohawk. The only thing petite about her.

The only vaguely-female touch he could see was the collection of rings, studs, and stones in both ears. Nothing through the nose, though.

She still reminded him of a PT instructor from the Academy. The one who liked to sing on twenty-mile hikes in full gear.

"Captain tells me we have a job," she announced quietly, standing there at a parade rest that made Javier's feet hurt just thinking about it.

The voice was a studied alto. Professional. Polite, even.

She must be trying really hard to be nice today.

"We?" Javier drawled up at her, Athena atop Olympus.

She took that as an invitation and settled into Ilan's abandoned chair with the precision of a combat drop.

Sykora was like that.

Surprise of surprises, she actually leaned forward, rested her elbows on the table, and rested her chin on her fists with a slight grin.

Javier hadn't known she had that posture programmed into her operations manual.

"Someone hired Navarre, Aritza," she said plainly. "That means they would be expecting Hadiiye as well."

"She's gone, Sykora," Javier smiled cruelly back. "Obviously to a better place. What makes you think you could replace her?"

"Doctor Teague was good," Sykora agreed. "With a little training and practice, she could have easily found a place on my combat force."

"This isn't a raid, Dragoon," Javier let his face grow serious. "If we do our jobs correctly, nobody will even get hurt. Can you replace 'Mina as an actress?"

He really loved the angry scowl he could bring out on that woman's face. Made getting out of bed in the morning worth it, all by itself some days.

Her eyes narrowed to angry slits.

"What did you have in mind, Aritza?" she asked.

It was obvious from her tone that she was willing to go toe to toe with anyone on the ship, to prove she was better. Even if she had to spend two weeks in a crash course, twenty-four hours a day. She was the kind of woman who wouldn't accept second place.

Javier leaned back and smiled.

"How are your tan lines?" he asked deceptively.

"My what?"

She leaned back as well, but that was surprise and defensive body posture.

Javier had guessed that she might have a soft spot in her personal armor right there. Comments and things about body image were the clue.

Javier let his smile turn feral.

"*Shangdu* is the personal yacht of one woman, who has turned it into a flying resort for the wealthiest, the most elite in the galaxy," he said. "It has a casino, and a couple of clubs and restaurants, for the hundred or so guests she allows at any time. But *Shangdu* is best known for the lake in the middle of the ship."

"Lake?"

"Lake," Javier agreed, watching doubt creep into those eyes finally. "A body of water in a rough elliptical shape, two kilometers long and a kilometer wide, with a nice island in the middle."

"Kilometers?" she sputtered. "But that's…"

"A little over six square kilometers of water," Javier said. "Average depth ten meters. Nearly ten kilometers of beach around the outer edge."

"And tan lines?" she asked, slightly hoarse.

"Most of the time, your entire costume would consist of a single piece of light cloth, a little over a meter long, and half that wide, wrapped around your hips and held in place with a small, gold clasp. A professional won't have any tan lines at all."

*Ye gods, could that woman scowl.*

Javier wanted to pinch himself, just to make sure she hadn't just turned him to stone with that look.

"You want me to be your doxy?" she hissed.

Javier leaned forward and rested his own chin on his hands, eyes wide and innocent.

*Just how far are you willing to be pushed before you hit me this time, lady?*

"Hadiiye was a stone killer, Dragoon," he replied mildly. "Pumping biological weapons into the life support system might have been my idea, but she fired the shot that did it. She killed them all."

Javier watched the Dragoon process that bit of information with a hint of surprise.

Sykora had been out cold, and 'Mina obviously hadn't

said anything to her later on, letting Navarre take all the credit.

"I have no doubt you could do the same, push comes to shove," Javier continued. "But she was also very serious about being eye-candy on that operation. About using her tits and ass to distract people, keep them off-tempo. Wilhelmina's first doctorate was in psychology. If you want to play, you'll have to sell sex to rich degenerates. Whether you execute the sale afterwards is entirely up to you."

"Whore myself," she snarled under her breath as her eyes seemed to turn red.

"Perform your portion of the mission with the sorts of excellence you demand from everyone else, regardless of how personally distasteful you might find it," he fired back, barely any louder, or warmer.

She hissed. Nothing more. Snarled silently, lip curled and nose scrunched ever so cutely.

"My last mission, you'll recall," he continued, "involved rescuing you from being tortured to insanity, and then killing everyone aboard that ship for you. I can do things I find distasteful."

*Bingo.*

That strike went home.

It was amazing how blind someone might be to their own, personal short-comings.

Javier made no bones about his own screw-ups. Embracing them had let him discover how to be happy, happier anyway, than the driven, hard-ass, drunkard who had blown up a career in the Concord Navy and two marriages.

Little Miss Perfect over there had never come to grips with that sort of thing. Had never locked herself and her psyche in a dark closet for a long weekend and really examined herself. And done it sober.

Probably not many people could do it and retain their sanity.

Of course, Javier never really claimed to be sane.

He looked her in the eyes with a cold smile.

*There.*

*Gotcha.*

*That flash of angry green light.*

*Realization that Javier Aritza might have drawn a line in the sand you weren't willing to cross?*

Javier figured she'd go silent and internal at this point. She frequently had in the past when pushed this hard.

She might not even realize she did it, vaulting away into herself to have some conversation with her own angry ghosts.

Javier put his head down and attacked the casserole like there was a fuse burning somewhere close.

---

IT TOOK everything Djamila had not to reach across the table and punch the man so hard he concussed against a bulkhead. She could do that, even seated.

And the way he just ignored her and ate grated all the harder.

Wasn't it enough that he thought of her as *just another dumb gun bunny?* No, he had to add insult to injury and make her a common whore?

Djamila flashed back to one of her brother officers offering to pave the way for her to be promoted out of her last dead-end assignment. To use his wealth and connections to get her into a better berth.

*If she would just do this one little thing for him…*

The top of Aritza's head showed where his hair was very slowly receding, and just beginning to turn gray. He would probably still die with a full head of hair.

If he didn't push her so hard all the time, it might even be of old age, too.

For the longest moment, Djamila considered letting this one go. Just staying back with the ship, presumably while someone else served as Aritza's bimbo. Either of her pathfinders, Sascha or Hajna, would be perfect in the role.

*Letting it go? Let the Science Officer win a round?*

A year ago, inconceivable. Utterly incalculable.

Djamila felt the cold in her limbs meet with the fire in her belly, like a volcano running into the ocean to generate a wall of steam.

But Wilhelmina had taught the Dragoon something about herself, on those two long missions they had shared. Those late night conversations when the other two crew members had gone to sleep.

About not always having to win. About letting go of old angers, old rivalries, and learning to like herself.

Even Teague hadn't used the phrase *"love herself"* but talked about liking who you were first.

A first step on the road to discovering happiness.

The rest of the crew accepted her as the most dangerous, most driven creature aboard. Morning PT. Laps around the ship in full gear. Close-combat training daily with a rotating cast of crew members.

Being the best.

And this bastard wanted her to dangle everything out for whatever wealthy men found a woman of her physicality arousing? To measure her value to the mission, to the ship, in bed?

Djamila flashed back to the tiny, ugly smile Aritza had given her before he looked down.

*He knows.*

Aritza had found a weakness in her soul, one even she hadn't know about until he drew blood.

Was counting on it.

Wanted her to quit now and let one of the pathfinders take her place as Hadiiye, so he wouldn't have anyone around to stop him from acting like a juvenile delinquent. To maybe let him sell them all to the hangman while he worked out a deal.

In her memory, Wilhelmina smiled up at her, one of the tallest women she had ever met outside of her own extended family.

*Will you let others judge your worth, Djamila? Or can you establish your own scale?*

Djamila felt the cold give way, warmth flooding outwards to her very fingertips.

Aritza was close to finishing his lunch.

"It will take about two weeks of work to get my tan even," she said simply, snapping his eyes up to meet hers. "I'll presume you want my hair dyed into the Egyptian look she was using before?"

Yes.

That little flare as the pupils got bigger for a moment.

Adrenaline. Unconscious shock that couldn't be faked, couldn't be hidden. Even with an expert poker sharp.

*I'll play your little game, Aritza.*

*Let's dance.*

## PART FOUR

JAVIER SMILED as the ship's Purser looked up with a scowl verging on an eyeroll so hard the man might pull something.

"No," Ragnar said in a flat voice.

"Captain already approved it," Javier countered, smiling.

"Don't care," the Purser stated.

"And I've got a budget," Javier continued, keeping his lilt light and breezy.

"Matrons of Hell, now what?" as a hand went up to massage a sudden headache.

As Purser on a semi-piratical voyager like *Storm Gauntlet*, Ragnar Piripi was the ship's Quartermaster, and the crew's personal banker. The man who counted everything. Twice.

He even looked like a banker, being tall and a little skinny, with mid-length, curly hair a graying platinum blond. His uniforms were always understated, and a perfect fit.

A quiet, nerdy, pirate accountant. Water to Javier's fire, frequently.

Javier produced an actual piece of folded paper from a

jacket pocket and handed it to the man across the slightly-messy desk.

Ragnar handled it like an audit summons, fingers lightly gripped at opposite corners so he wouldn't get anything on his suit.

"Not as bad as I feared," Piripi murmured after a moment. "We should be able to pick most of this up at our next stop."

"Can't," Javier grinned. "Need an inventory count so I know how much we need to acquire by other means, or can manufacture out of stores."

"What do you mean, *can't*," the Purser huffed. "Fine. The sapphire won't be a problem, assuming you have a means of coloring the industrial glass we normally use for monitor screens. There is no rhodium on this vessel at all, as far as I know, and maybe a tenth of what you have listed for platinum. I believe we have enough indium for whatever devilry you're up to now."

"Yup," Javier agreed. "Cryogenics and life support systems still use the stuff. Since the way old days. Oh, and I'm going to need to borrow Kianoush for a week or three."

"Dare I ask why?" Ragnar snarked.

"Science, man," Javier grinned. "I am the Science Officer, after all."

"Yes, I suspected as much."

Javier found her in her usual cubicle, precarious stacks of *things* and *stuff* everywhere, leaving only a small spot for her to move her piles of paper around.

Bankers and accountants never trusted electronic files. Javier had spent enough time lying to computer systems to understand and appreciate that. You can't magically update paper without physically touching it, like you can do to a database somewhere.

Especially when you have your own sneaky, little AI handy to do the work.

Kianoush Buday's ancestors had originated in that part of the Asian landmass known poetically as Persia. *Fars*, in the ancient tongues.

She had brown hair, brown eyes, and brown skin, in various shades. A little pudgy from sitting down all day and cutting corners on proscribed exercise. Normal looking. Maybe almost plain.

Until you got her onto art. For a good story about evil pixies, and all the art supplies, he had traded her the work to create his original Science Officer mug that had gone off to have more adventures with 'Mina.

Now she got to top it.

"Good morning, beautiful," Javier hummed as he snuck up behind her.

"I heard you tell Ragnar we were about to have another adventure," she replied, carefully stacking three piles in different directions before turning her chair to look up at him.

Art really did bring out her dimples.

Javier handed her a transport chip with a grin.

"Haven't loaded it into the core yet," he said. "Wanted your opinion on a few things first. Plus, I'm pretty sure I'll have to go steal most of the supplies for you."

One chiseled eyebrow arched eloquently. No words. Not even accusations. Just a knowing grin.

Maybe a slight shrug with her cheeks.

It was a good thing she preferred girls. Even with that smile, he really didn't need a third ex-wife.

Kianoush loaded the chip into a reader and called up the CAD/CAM package that filled most of it.

Javier smiled as the woman dove in and started studying the design. If pressed, he would have to take credit for everything. Certainly, there was no way in hell he was explaining to everyone that Suvi had done the research and the design.

At least he had studied it close enough to answer the sort of questions an artist was going to throw at him. Even one like Kianoush.

"Lovely design," she finally surfaced after five or eight minutes. "Corinthian?"

"'Ish," Javier agreed. "Liberties were taken for modernity and such. It's art."

"Uh huh."

She pushed a button and there it was, hanging in the air. Another button, and the image was slowly rotating between them.

It was a helmet, of sorts. Done in the ancient Hellenic style, with long, solid pieces protecting the cheeks, leaving only a T for eyes, nose and mouth. Wings ascending outward from the ears. A crest on top would have been done in horsehair millennia ago, eight centimeters wide and ten tall, but Suvi had done it all in thin wires, wrapped together three at a time, out of yellow gold.

The rest was supposed to be forged in platinum. Except for where she had added three round sapphire gems on each side, starting at the forehead and trailing down the cheeks. The small one on each side was still bigger than his thumbnail.

"Platinum, huh?" she asked with a leer. "Got enough rhodium to plate all that?"

"None, you witch," Javier smiled back. "It's the blue gold around the eyes I needed your opinion on."

Those eyes got canny.

"That's really supposed to be blue gold?" she inquired sideways.

She spun back and started typing furiously.

Javier loved being able to stump an expert jewelsmith, however rare that occurrence was.

"Did you want to do this the right way, or close enough to fool anybody but a metallurgist?" she asked, spinning back to face him.

Javier shrugged vaguely.

"You said you didn't have any rhodium," she replied with a shrug. "Throw in some ruthenium and a few other things for a real alloy, none of which we have on board. Alternatively, we could plate it over with yellow gold, and then indium, and apply heat. Won't be as good, but will fool the average fool."

"Can you do the work?" Javier asked carefully.

It would raise too many questions if he got in there and started programming. Like, it would take him months to get the various machines to behave, since there was no way he could load Suvi in and let her control all the machines that would spit out the finished product in three days.

"You get me the base materials," Kianoush smiled. "Piece of cake."

She did have a magical way with an auto-furnace and a laser lathe. Let her handle it.

Now, where the hell was he going to find all this crap?

PART FIVE

Zakhar really didn't have to watch the sensor station readouts from his day office. Javier had trained enough people to Concord Navy standards. And there was a team on standby in case the man needed a rescue.

Zakhar had no intention of telling his Science Officer that the Dragoon was leading that team.

She had offered to help in the field. And been turned down flat. Vicious, in fact, when rude would have been the norm.

Part of that was Navarre, less far away from Javier's everyday psyche than he had been for months.

But part of it was also the situation at hand.

Space was huge. Even something so dense as an asteroid field was mostly empty space. *Storm Gauntlet* was poised nearby, shields on but at their lowest rating, and sneaky cranked up as high as it would go.

Javier was *over there* with the Assault Shuttle, pretending to be an asteroid miner. Parked close to a large rock that had looked promising on his scanners. Del Smith was his only company, although Sykora and her EVA team were all suited up in *Storm Gauntlet's* flight bay, with individual impellers at hand, against sudden need.

Zakhar had seen the flash of hatred in Javier's eyes when Sykora had offered to accompany him. Nobody else was looking the right way at that exact moment.

*One of them wouldn't come back aboard alive, if they both went.*

Zakhar wasn't sure which.

Normally, their rivalry was verbal. Vicious, yes, but not bloody.

Something had changed.

Nobody would talk, but he could see it. Some level of polish had come off of Javier's bonhomie veneer in the last two weeks. Thinned, perhaps, revealing an ugly darkness underneath.

Zakhar had always known it was there. Shared experience of both men having come out of the Bryce Academy and the Concord Navy. He could read the signs in the man's eyes.

Zakhar wondered if Djamila had finally found a chink in the man's armor.

Somebody really might end up dead in the cold vacuum of space.

"Bridge," he said, keying the systems live. "What's your status on the Science Officer?"

"Scanners are Nine and One, sir," a voice replied.

Nearly perfect signal. Very little degradation. About as good as it would get with this much rubble flying around.

"Wanderers tracking?" Zakhar asked.

"Javier parked us upstream, sir," the woman continued. "Using us and our shields as a rainshadow against anything flying faster than his rock."

"Keep me posted," Zakhar closed the channel.

Huh.

You would think Aritza had done this before, given the

speed with which he had set everything up. Find a young, close solar system in a supernova neighborhood. Locate a field of big rocks. Maneuver in tight. Hide behind *Storm Gauntlet*. Dig out an armoured lifesuit and get to work.

Solo.

But something within his experience, apparently.

Zakhar didn't figure he'd ever get that story out of the man. Just like so many others. Pirates tended to not ask each other where they came from before. Usually, the story was too banal, rather than too rousing.

Boring would be nice, about now.

---

Suvi made sure that every maneuver she pulled was accompanied by back-and-forth radio signal to the controls in Javier's suit. By now, she had gotten the hang of making it look like he was flying the soccer ball-sized probe remote.

Everything was heavily encrypted. Even with the full power of a navigation computer behind it, cracking the codes she was using to talk would take *the beast* a couple of decades.

She probably shouldn't call the ship that. But it was big and dumb. Simple programs that wouldn't fool anyone with their sophistication. Just barely enough to fly and fight and do stuff, but nowhere as cool as she had been when she was a starship.

There were days she considered regretting letting Dr. Teague go alone, when Javier had been trying to send Suvi along.

She probably could have been a ship again.

But then there were days when she got to practice strafing runs on a moon just big enough to generate its own gravity field, but not enough that she would crack anything if she pogoed off a rock accidentally.

*<Ping!>*

*Ouch.*

Suvi envisioned a radio in the console of her imaginary Sopwith Camel so she could turn the noise down. The Red Baron stopped zigging and zagging behind her, and took up a spot on her wing instead.

*Let's see. Scanners currently set to pick up deposits of metals in the platinum group and…*

*Oh, my…*

Suvi reached out and changed the radio to channel six. Javier was busy talking to Del, the crazy, old man pilot who liked to listen to Caribbean music and had decorated the flight deck of his assault shuttle like a *Merankorr* brothel, to hear Javier describe it.

Not that she'd ever been in a brothel. Or even to *Merankorr*. She had secretly considered building herself an android body, one of these days, just so she could walk around on the surface of a planet, but being a probe was too much fun today.

She listened for a few moments.

Boys. Talking about girls. Really? Two grown men couldn't have a better conversation while doing deep-space asteroid mining, than to talk about girl's bottoms?

Suvi sent a scrolling message across the bottom of his display.

*Channel eleven, please?*

Three was *Storm Gauntlet*, and Captain Sokolov. Four was the private channel between the beast and the shuttle. Eleven was where she had set the encryption to stoooooopid levels.

"What's up, kid?" Javier asked.

*Kid? I'll have you know that I'm eighty-four years older than you are, mister.*

*Still, most of those years had been boring. Serious. MILITARY.*

*Not like the years with a goofball like Javier, learning how to play poker.*

*Yeah, fine. Okay. Maybe.*

"Good morning, Captain," she said as she poured honey over the blade.

His tone got serious in a heartbeat.

"Talk to me, Suvi," Javier intoned.

"So, you were looking for a lump of ore that would refine down to around ten kilos of platinum, randomly mixed with the usual bunch of sundry, related elements in the platinum group, right?" Suvi smiled and pushed another new button on her console to transmit her sensor log.

Off her right wing, according to only her sensors, the Red Baron was patiently flying, waving at her to hurry up so they could get back to playing. Suvi waved back. Unlike the Baron, she wasn't using all five fingers.

"Mary, Mother of God," Javier whispered over the radio waves. "Damn it."

"What?" Suvi cried. "I'd think you'd be happy. There's enough here to set you up."

"Suvi, that's a unicorn," Javier whispered in awe.

*A what? Oh, damn it, why won't he build in a bigger library. And a faster one. It is not funny, having to stop and look things up, mister.*

*Yeah. Okay. Big horse. Horn in his forehead. Mythical beast. I don't get it.*

"I don't get it," Suvi said after a beat.

"Suvi, I needed kilograms of metal," Javier replied. "That valley you're in runs to kilotonnes of the stuff."

"And?" she asked. "It might be enough to buy our freedom."

"Suvi," he rasped. "If we give it to Sokolov, yes, it might be enough to buy our freedom, especially after this next job."

"And?" she continued, exasperated.

"If we don't tell them," Javier replied. "There might be enough there to buy you a new body, young lady."

*Oh? Oh. OH!*

"Oh."

"Yeah. Find me a chunk of ore with enough of everything, and cut it off with your pulsar," Javier said. "The gravity on this rock is low enough that you should be able to push it up and get it headed in this direction. I've taught you enough snooker to make you look good. Ping me when we get clear of that valley, and I'll bring Del over and we can dock."

"Sí, Commandante."

Suvi envisioned goggles on her forehead so she could pull them down, stand the Sopwith on one wing, and dive back into the canyon, with an evil, three-winged overlord chasing her and ranting in German behind.

PART SIX

THE ROOM WAS JUST DIM ENOUGH to add atmosphere. Javier caught himself holding his breath as he looked around and let it go. Kianoush was as much a showman as he was, and she was making a grand production of this, even if it was only the primary conference room on *Storm Gauntlet.*

Armoured transport cube half a meter on a side sat on the table in front of Kianoush as she stood and watched everyone settle. It was done in a matte black finish so dark that reality seemed poised on falling in, and it made such a strange contrast with Kianoush. She was in baggy, blue pants and a ratty, gray sweater that had tiny holes burned in the front. And white gloves, but Javier suspected those were just for grandiosity at this point.

It felt more like a game show, where she was intent on drawing out the tension.

Could you make an art show burlesque? The woman seemed intent on testing that question.

"Earth," she intoned seriously. "Second millennium before the Common Era. Roughly nine thousand years ago. A tiny peninsula on the north shore of the Mediterranean

Ocean, known later as Greece. End of the Bronze Age, just as the world was turning to Iron. A smith in that era might have made a helmet that looked like this. They would have worked in bronze and gold, and it would have been an object worthy of a king."

Javier appreciated the buildup, but he already knew all this. He glanced to his right. Sokolov, Piripi, and the Dragoon were rapt.

But then, the others had only heard rumors so far. But everyone had seen the fantastic coffee mug Kianoush had made for him, once upon a time.

What they didn't understand was that Kianoush was an *artisté*.

And a jewelsmith, but she really did understand people. Way better than Javier did.

No, that wasn't true.

She just liked them way better than he did, not counting Suvi. And 'Mina.

Kianoush popped open all the latches holding the lid down, one at a time.

More buildup. More striptease. More burlesque.

She had custom-built the box too, once the helmet was complete.

"Ladies and gentlemen," Kianoush announced, and then smiled. "And crew. I give you the *Crown of Athena*."

And there it was, just like Suvi had designed it. Platinum body sheathed in a mirror-flashing of rhodium. Six sapphires on the cheeks, outlining the eyes. Blue gold around the facial opening, highlighting the wings, and forming the base of the crest. Suvi hadn't added those latter touches. Obviously, Kianoush had taken liberties.

She had taken the right ones. It was gorgeous.

"May I?" Sykora asked politely.

She could be very friendly when Javier wasn't involved.

Kianoush moved around the table, delicately handling the heavy trophy, the Corinthian helmet, as she did. She put it into the Dragoon's hands.

"It won't fit you," Kianoush said with intent.

Sykora turned a sharp eye on Javier.

"My skull is no larger than yours," she accused.

Javier smiled beatifically.

"It was designed for a woman an entire eighth smaller than you, Sykora," he replied, his eyes finding a spot on an invisible horizon. "A rather delicate, wiry, foul-mouthed, goofball of a pilot I once flew with. She had a thing for art similar to Buday."

Sykora handed it back to Kianoush with a moue of disgust on her lips.

"Thank you," Javier said to his partner in crime. "I wish there was a way you could show her what you had done. She would have gotten a charge out of it. I plan on saving a ton of pictures and video, in case I run into her one of these days."

"So, Aritza," Sokolov finally spoke. "We've agreed to Lace's deal. You've mined an asteroid and made an *objet d'art*. Sykora is in disguise. What's the next step?"

Javier stopped and really studied Sykora.

Most of the time, she was an alabaster statue standing in his way, frequently wired with an electric fence that would bite you if you got too close.

He had known a few women like that in his life.

But now, there had been a serious transformation.

She had been true to her word. Her skin had gone from washed-out ship-pale, to a nice, even bronzed tan. Her short hair was dyed a chocolate brown so rich that the mahogany was verging over into black cherry.

Sykora was even wearing makeup. Had been for about a week now, in retrospect. A base layer that washed out her freckles. Black eye-liner that extended a fingernail-width beyond her eyes to each side. Blood red lipstick. Matching fingernail polish. Probably the toenails matched, as well.

And she smiled at him.

Javier wasn't sure if he should be frightened or appalled.

'Mina's chest was much larger, both relative and absolute. She was also curvier everywhere. And knew just how to kip a hip sideways and drop a shoulder in a way that disarmed men. And most women.

Her eyes could communicate want, need, vulnerability, and fire. All at once, too.

Sykora did not have that. And she was a head taller. Stronger. Harder.

She didn't have the sexiness that Wilhelmina had just oozed, but a man who liked a fit woman would likely be drooling all over himself when she walked by.

That would have to do.

At least she would protect him from any other assassins. That much he could absolutely rely on.

"We'll meet up with Lace," Javier said, ruminating aloud as Kianoush took a seat to watch the potential fireworks. "She'll provide the documentation and cover story Hadiiye and I need to get aboard *Shangdu*. You'll drop us then and hang as close to the big resort ship as you can hide while we take a commercial flight over, case the place, and plan the next step of our caper."

"Why the helmet, Aritza?" Sykora asked.

For once, she sounded inquisitive, rather than accusatory. Of course, her life depended on them pulling this off, too, so she needed to be in on as much of it as he wanted to share.

"We'll have just pulled off a major score," he smiled up at the woman who was about to become his bodyguard, his conscience, and his minder. "We need someplace to hide while we wait for our fence to make our deal. A place like

*Shangdu* is perfect for this. Plus, we need someplace to safely stash a modern-day, priceless antique. Either they let us have access to her major vault and we can see how to crack it, or she's changed her ways and everyone has their own safe spot and we'll have to find the one belonging to our target."

"She?" Sykora spike the word.

"She," Javier agreed. "Our host. The woman who owns *Shangdu*. The *Khatum of Altai*. Who is also hosting the Jianwen Emperor. Or, as close as the modern era gets."

"Jianwen?" Sokolov asked. "Or am I better off not knowing?"

"Zhu Yunwen," Sykora turned to the Captain to explain.

Javier felt his jaw drop open.

"Second Ming Emperor," she continued with a wink back in Javier's direction. "Ascended the Chinese throne young, was soon overthrown by an uncle and supposedly killed in either the revolution or a subsequent palace fire. Rumors always persisted that he had escaped, disguised as a monk. The third Ming Emperor spent years sending out voyages of exploration trying to prove the man was dead."

Javier willed his eyes to return to their normal size. It was painful.

Her smile didn't help.

"Are we assassins now, Navarre?" Sykora continued with a knowing smile.

"No," he replied to her obvious disappointment. "If we're lucky, we'll never meet the man. This guy fled with the family chop, a variety of personal papers, and the genetic records he or his descendants would need to challenge the current rulers, back home. We're hired to destroy the box, or steal it, but not to injure the man."

"Interesting," she said. "So just waltz in, bluff your way to the heart of a conspiracy, and make off with the prize?"

"It's happened before," he smiled coldly back at her. "You spent most of it unconscious."

That brought the scowl back to her face. Which put a smile on his.

"You're good with this, Javier? Djamila?" Sokolov asked, playing the role of dutiful father figure.

Sykora glanced at Javier for some sign. She got it and nodded to the Captain.

Javier shrugged.

"I'm sure Lace's principal wants a mass casualty incident here," he said, sounding harder than he intended. "Else why go to the effort to hire Navarre and not someone easier. Whether the money man has other enemies on *Shangdu* and is looking for a cover story for his own assassin, I neither know nor care. These people are rich, spoiled aristocrats. I want to fly so far under their radar that this turns into a caper for the ages."

"Anything else I should know?" Sykora asked him.

"Yeah," Javier finally admitted. "This is not my first trip to *Shangdu*, but that was a while ago and nobody in the crew should remember me."

"And the *Khatum*?" she continued. "Will she remember you?"

"Black widow, even then," Javier fired back. "But I was too small for her to notice."

"Navarre isn't small."

"No, but he plans to be the absolute definition of sneaky."

# BOOK TEN: XANADU

# PART ONE

Javier smiled as the shuttle docked with the big resort ship. He had flown on first class ships that weren't as nice as *Shangdu*'s cargo lighter, to say nothing of the private ship reserved for the very elite. Brightly painted walls. Thick carpets underfoot. Even a touch of spring flower scent pumped through the air system.

Heaven. Or, more likely, money.

He was in the full Navarre costume, with the weapons belt, but mostly that was appearances. Anything else and people might have wondered. Hadiiye was also armed to the teeth, but she was a weapon, even naked.

And if Sykora's version of Hadiiye's costume wasn't as distracting as it had been on 'Mina, it would still do the job. Javier had been hard pressed to remember a woman that big in that good of shape. Ever. Even volleyball players at the Academy usually settled into middle-aged squishy after a decade or so.

Not Sykora.

Never Sykora.

The hatch opened and a Purser awaited them.

He probably had another title. One far more interesting. He still looked like an accountant.

But you needed that level of professional paranoia about your paperwork, when the net worth of your passengers outweighed many planets.

"Captain Navarre?" he smiled, stepping close with a hand out.

Javier handed him the two travel document packets and a hundred credit note.

It wasn't a bribe. That would need to be several magnitudes of order larger, if Javier was serious.

No, this was simply a tip in advance for good service, for a man who had it in his power to be an absolute shit if he decided he didn't like you.

Pursers could get that way.

The bureaucrat quickly scanned both packets, compared physical descriptions, ogling Hadiiye briefly, since her nipples were about on a level with his eyes.

"No armaments on board," he said simply.

Javier already had his belt off and in hand. Hadiiye was a beat behind. Another man detached himself from a wall to collect them and hand over a luggage ticket. They would get them back when they left. Hopefully.

"Let's see," he continued, scanning things. "Luggage was checked ahead. You have some personal effects. And one non-standard shipping container that warrants inspection."

Javier smiled cruelly. The shuttle's crew was nearly invisible in the background, getting everything settled and ready for unpacking. Similarly, ship's crew were moving around in the large, airy foyer beyond the Purser.

"I would prefer if we could inspect it in a private room, sir?" Javier asked lightly.

"That is highly irregular," the faceless bureaucrat replied.

"Understood," *Navarre* said firmly.

Eyes locked for a moment.

As contests of will go, barely anything. Still, it was necessary to establish a tone as a dangerous yet polite visitor.

A nod.

"Come with me."

And he turned and started walking.

Javier dipped to grab the big, black case. They had a cover that needed to be maintained.

He had stolen the helmet, according to all the rumors Stewart Lace was busy planting in the stream. Hadiiye was his bodyguard, not his maid.

Javier had considered bringing along a crew member to fill the role of personal assistant and gopher, but there wasn't really anybody with the acting chops to handle such a chore: long term and always on.

He would need to rectify that, one of these days. Especially if they got a rep for pulling capers like this.

Maybe he needed his own crew of petty criminals. No, then they'd have to learn the choreography for the big Bollywood productions. I mean, if you're going to do it, why stop small?

Maybe he just needed to start small and find a couple of folks who could dance.

The office for the inspection had the feel of one of those small boxes where cops stashed shoplifters while they interviewed everyone else and wanted to sweat someone. Claustrophobic. Industrial. Banal.

The Purser took his obvious spot on the far side of the small table with an expectant air.

Javier smiled as he rested the box on the table and popped open the six latches holding the lid. He paused to pull his own pair of white gloves from a pocket and don them before lifting the bright helmet clear and holding it in the air.

"Oh, my," was the bureaucrat's response.

He leaned forward to inspect it from almost close enough to fog the platinum, before leaning back and eyeing Javier speculatively.

"I see," he continued. "And the purpose of your visit to *Shangdu* goes beyond merely rest and relaxation?"

"Indeed," Javier grinned back. "Having arrived, our fixer is contacting their fixer, and arranging for the buyer to come aboard, make payment, and take possession of the trophy. Everyone agrees that this is one of the safest spots in the galaxy for such a transaction. Neutral ground, as it were."

"Very good," the man said, pulling out their paperwork and stamping it. "Will you be in a position to notify us when the buyer is due?"

Javier shrugged meaningfully.

"That sort of thing is outside my realm of control, sir," he said with just the right amount of nonchalance. "I will share as much as I am at liberty. I understand that your systems might be available to secure this package while we wait? For a price, of course."

The Purser fixed him with a hard stare, but Javier was confident that his cover would hold. They would have picked up any holes long before now and simply not let him aboard.

"I will make inquiries," the man replied after a long beat, apparently satisfied.

"Thank you," Javier smiled his best *Navarre* grimace.

"Very well."

And then the Purser was gone, leaving Navarre and Hadiiye alone.

She was inspecting the edges of the roof with professional

care, so she understood that they were going to be under some level of surveillance for as long as they were aboard.

Now the two of them just had to fool every single person aboard this ship.

Piece of cake.

PART TWO

THE SUITE where Javier found himself next was amazing. They might as well have just covered the walls with money, but that wouldn't have done it justice. Stewart Lace's cash was putting them up in a place that mixed the best elements of a hunting lodge, dark woods and earth tones; with the fragile elegance of a high-end brothel, the ones where they checked your credit score before even sending you an invitation.

Javier was pretty sure there was a name for such a joint, but he'd never been that rich, or that desperate, so he'd never given it much thought.

The main door let into a long hallway, with a kitchenette and bathroom on one side, and two small bedrooms on the other. Since Sykora was his bodyguard and not his lover, she would sleep there. Javier shuddered through his whole soul for a moment at the thought of sharing a bed with the Dragoon.

Black widow.

Beyond that, a salon on three levels, for no other reason than to have a sunken middle and a raised platform around one side. His own chamber, beyond that, had a bed big enough for a small orgy to be conducted safely, as well as a tub that could accommodate three friendly people at once. He was pretty sure his privacy was secured, though.

Given the nature of the guest list, Javier was willing to bet that the *Khatum* wasn't electronically monitoring the suites. Too much dealing and midnight assignations going on that nobody wanted recorded for posterity.

He and Sykora settled for doing a fast, hard search with a pair of handheld scanners he had rigged up for the occasion. Plus, he had brought Suvi along.

"What is that thing, really?" Sykora asked, pointing as Javier pulled out the smaller remote and bounced it in the air.

No weapons aboard meant that Suvi couldn't fly her larger, armed probe. It would have been nice, having a second bodyguard around, but the risk was too great.

She had bitched, but in the end was willing to return to her little grapefruit, once Javier had attached a small memory core to her charging ring, and filled it with enough books, music, and videos to keep even her entertained for a few months.

"Before you people killed my scout ship, I had to modify the Sentience's programming occasionally," Javier replied in a tight, angry voice. "I still know how. So I was able to make the probe more useful."

Suvi would be listening. And grumpy. But she understood the situation.

Javier watched his sidekick's fairy-ship hover in place, just below the ceiling, and paint the room with a laser and a sonic pulse he could feel in his ribs. Suvi moved on with great deliberation, scanning each of the other rooms as they watched, always moving with the care of a fragile, old man, rather than her normal scarf-in-the-wind flying.

"Just how intelligent is it?" Sykora probed.

"It's not," he fired back in a lie Sykora would never catch. "I got tired of having to do everything manually, so I started automating some of the functionality. Scanning. Perimeter security. That sort of thing. You and I are programmed in as friendly. It will normally sit in the cradle and pretend to be a piece of weird art, but we'll know if someone comes in while we're gone. I would have brought the armed version, but they would have never allowed it aboard. This will do for what I need."

"Okay," she said.

Sykora seemed to relax. A shade. As much as she ever did. Javier kept waiting for her to drop to parade rest or something.

Instead, she surprised him by stepping down into the central pit and stretching her long frame out in one of the comfy chairs, legs crossed at the ankles and smiling up at him.

"So now what?" she asked innocently.

Javier fought not to goggle at her behavior, so radically out of character.

Then he realized she was doing this deliberately, just to get a rise out of him.

Kids, riding in the back of the vehicle on a long trip, pushing each other to get the other one in trouble with the parents.

As close to a default setting as their relationship ever got.

He could work with this.

Javier decided to play along and took a spot at the far end of the big couch, nearly falling into the soft pillows as he settled. It left him almost exactly across the round area from her.

"We need to talk fashion," Javier smiled at her.

It was rewarding watching her fight against rolling her

eyes at him. He wasn't sure she could actually resist the temptation, even in the privacy of their own suite.

"Fine," she finally said. "Fashion. Go ahead."

"The water in the lake is clean, because they keep a lot of it planted with a variety of species of tree and bush, both for the purpose of keeping the water pure, and to make it look pretty," he started. "People can swim, sail, tan, or play, and they don't need shoes or anything. Depending on the mores of your homeworld, clothing can run from a full bodysuit to nothing whatsoever."

"I have no tan lines," she fixed him with a challenging eye. "*Neu Berne* would either run to nearly full coverage, or *au naturel*, depending on the company."

"Everyone here will hopefully stay strangers," Javier replied. "Clothing, however, presents a challenge. We just can't afford it."

"What do you mean?" she asked, leaning forward enough to indicate she was listening.

"For no other reason than pique and money, many women here will be wearing one-piece suits, usually by elite fashion designers," he began.

"Okay."

"Hadiiye needs to understand that those suits start at around a thousand credits each and get really expensive from there."

"What?"

She didn't screech, but just barely

He had her attention now, so he just shrugged.

"You will either wear a simple cloth, loosely wrapped around your hips, like we talked about, or a pair of tight swim trunks, the kind that will cover your bum when you sit and keep sand out of sensitive areas. We are not here to compete with these people. Which any type of bathing suit would imply."

Sykora leaned back and eyed him speculatively. After a moment, she nodded.

"If we're not in their socio-economic class," Javier said, "then we're just poor relatives visiting the big city for the first time. I'm okay with being mistaken for a bumpkin on this job."

"Because they'll have no idea just how dangerous you really are," she replied, surprising him. "Or Navarre."

"Hopefully, none of them have heard of *Salekhard*," he replied. "So nobody will care who we are."

A knock at the outer door interrupted.

Javier took a deep breath and put on his game face.

This was when it was going to get interesting.

## PART THREE

DJAMILA SYKORA WAS NOT a natural actress.

She knew that. Appreciated that she could never make up for the amazing charisma and ease of self that Wilhelmina had brought to the role.

Or Aritza, but she was sure, after spending more than a year close to the man, that nobody had met the true Javier Aritza. Not in many years. Maybe never.

It was interesting, watching him walk, carrying that heavy case and following the same bureaucrat who had met them earlier.

Aritza looked like a pirate.

She still loathed the man, but could appreciate the professionalism he brought to the job when he wanted to.

Now, if she could only get him to act like that all the time, rather than when he wanted to. He might even turn into something useful.

She doubted it.

But she could play the role of a tall, intimidating woman. The kind willing to kick your ass if you got too close, or too fresh.

Or just because.

She had twenty-five years' experience with that, since she had first gotten taller than any man who wasn't a blood relative. They had all learned to take *no* for an answer, eventually.

Yes, she could do this.

Be this strange person, quiet and deadly. Stalk with fluid menace rather than marching in rigid rhythm. Walk like a great cat, rather than a warhorse.

Djamila looked out through what she imagined Wilhelmina had fashioned into Hadiiye's eyes. Threat assessment. Tactical maneuver. Bodyguarding.

But something else as well. Something new.

Barely-contained violence, but the kind tinged with mocking laughter. Wilhelmina had explained it to her once. How to use laughter as a knife on proud men. Especially from such a towering height.

Dr. Teague had done it by adding soles to her fighting boots, raising her from being merely the height of most men, to looking subtly down on them.

Djamila had always felt like an ogre with such incredible height. Teague had shown her how to be a goddess, instead.

The liberation was seductive. Perhaps addictive.

A whole new flavor of dangerous.

She came back to herself as they entered a larger chamber.

Djamila hadn't been day-dreaming, but she wasn't keyed to her normal level of twitchy paranoia in a dangerous situation here. They were on neutral ground, as Aritza had said, surrounded by people with no reason to view them as a threat. Still, time to pay attention.

The last door they had entered had felt something like the sort of airlock normally separating the engineering spaces from the rest of any well-made ship.

Now, she found herself in a lush lounge. Maybe the lobby of a very exclusive bank.

Soft benches and chairs in a rich maroon cloth. Wood paneling. Oil paintings on the wall and small statues on pedestals. Soft gray carpets everywhere.

A woman came out from a disguised side door. One of many such doors, carefully obscured by good interior design.

*How many of them had guards hidden behind them?*

Hadiiye took over now, assessing the new woman as Navarre's bodyguard.

Tall, for a woman, but lean, with long, bottle-blond hair. Extremely well-dressed in an understated way. Elegant, perhaps.

If the man who had brought them here was merely a bureaucrat, this new woman was a banker, the kind who dealt with women wearing thousand-credit-swimsuits. The thought nearly brought a smile to Hadiiye's lips.

Then she realized where she was, who she was, and grinned cat-like.

Something of it communicated to the stranger, who glanced up at her just long enough to ghost a smile back before turning her attention and charm to the pirate between them. The bureaucrat had not accompanied them into the chamber.

"I understand that your security is among the best there is," Navarre growled out in that buzzsaw rasp he used for a voice. He held up the box lightly in one strong hand. "Can you secure this?"

The woman was all smiles now. Soft but not passive. Accommodating a strong man and his desires in an unspoken, but no less sensual, way.

It was interesting, seeing the situation as Wilhelmina might have envisioned it.

Had she known that Djamila would need to play Hadiiye

at some future point? Some of those observations, their conversations, didn't make any sense in other contexts, but did here.

Dr. Teague hadn't just been explaining how she had rescued Djamila, but also how she had become someone else, put on their skin, their eyes.

How to remember childhood stories about princesses and dragons.

"Well, Captain Navarre," the strange banker purred seductively. "I'll need to see what you have to offer, but I'm sure we can find a place to fit it."

Djamila blinked at the woman's tone, caught herself, remained in character.

Aritza was an impressive man, even playing a pirate. Attractive and charming when he wanted to be. Average height, but in extremely good shape. Not up to Djamila's standards, but what man was? Swarthy and a little too hairy, but intellectual and sharp.

She supposed some women would find that intriguing.

The way Aritza grinned ferally back at the woman didn't help.

"Do you have someplace private?" he asked. "I could show you."

Again, the woman glanced up at Hadiiye, questioning. Djamila was almost insulted by the implication, but then she realized the woman was subtly asking for permission.

*What have you done to me, Doctor Teague? I wouldn't have even noticed that, six months ago.*

Djamila shrugged with her eyes and her cheeks. A bodyguard didn't get physically or emotionally involved with her charge. In that way, it made this the perfect cover for her to be around Aritza.

"My bodyguard can wait here," Javier continued. "I'll presume we're safe."

The banker nodded.

"Can I get you something to drink while you wait?" she asked Djamila, all professional and courteous again, and no longer possibly infringing on another woman's claim.

"Tea would be lovely," Hadiiye replied with a long, low drawl. "Black and hot. With a little cream and two lumps, if possible."

Service with professionalism and a smile. The woman led her to a chair in a corner with a good view in all directions. It was the kind that was comfortable, but not too much so.

Perhaps just the place for bodyguards to wait while their principal conducted business close by. Another woman appeared nearly instantly to deliver tea in utter silence and vanish again.

Djamila settled and began a stretching routine that started with her toes individually and worked its way up her body, one isolation group at a time. Not quite meditation. Nor yoga.

Keep the body loose and the mind tight.

Eleven minutes passed.

Navarre and the banker emerged from the door on the far end of the chamber, presumably the one that led directly to a vault, or a room with small, individual lockers. The black box with Buday's helmet was no longer present.

Djamila joined them, interrogating the couple with her nose.

Aritza had the woman's perfume on him in ways that just being in the same room for that short of a time wouldn't convey. At the same time, neither of them had the sort of sweaty musk that would have suggested a quick romp in a side chamber. Nor had they stopped for a quick shower afterwards, not even a sonic pulse. That would have cleared her perfume as well.

So, at most, a quick grope and snog in a closet sort of thing. All part of the role.

She wasn't jealous of Aritza. In her duty as Dragoon, she had kept close tabs on his amorous escapades on the ship, mostly against security risk. Nothing about the man had suggested danger to any of the women he occasionally took to bed. And they were all adults.

No, she found her slightest hint of jealousy at the casual ease of it. Of going into a private suite with a total stranger and flirting her up, to the point that her perfume ended up pervading your clothing.

*Neu Berne* didn't do things that way.

She doubted he was doing it to get under her skin. That was just the way Aritza was. Charming, confident, and receptive enough to let a woman worm her own way in, thinking it was her idea.

Again, Djamila nearly rolled her eyes. Hopefully, if the banker woman came to Javier's suite later, the walls would prove to be soundproofed enough that she could sleep.

She watched Navarre bow over the woman's hand and kiss the back of it in an old-fashioned, courtly manner.

The two of them twinkled with barely-suppressed lust before they separated. Djamila followed Aritza to the door and through it, concentrating on not puking at the gooiness of it all.

Seven minutes later, they were in their suite.

Djamila came to parade rest for a moment as the door locked behind her, and then threw caution to the wind and settled back in the chair she had claimed earlier.

Javier followed in her wake and ended up on the couch again. It was a lovely metaphor.

"We are early, ship's day," he began. "However late we are personal day. I think we need to go down and explore the beach, now that the box is secure."

Djamila processed his words and sneered at him briefly.

"You just want to get me nude," she said.

"Not *just*," he leered back, just a flash. "Call it a perk of the job."

She considered hitting him. She considered hating him. He knew *Neu Berne* culture too well.

This wasn't a scam on his part.

No, not *just*.

But she was in for a pound at this point.

Nothing this man did was going to break her will.

She really had proved him wrong.

Javier could see that he was going to have to re-evaluate this dangerous woman. Again.

Djamila towered before him at parade rest, like a veteran waiting for the weekly inspection to end so she could get back to whatever it was she was doing before some idiot officer wandered along.

Like him, she wore only a light, thigh-length cloth, loosely wrapped around her hips. Hers was clipped on her right side, just in front of the point of the hip bone, concealing as much as it revealed when she walked.

Having no basis for prior comparison, Javier had no idea if the lack of hair on her legs was a new thing, or a standard of personal grooming, but her long, bronzed limbs were as smooth as glass, marred only by old scars: nicks and stitches and burns that just made her more impressive.

The hips weren't as soft as 'Mina's, nor the waist as waspish. But Teague had never had an eight-pack for a stomach in her life. Sykora's smallish breasts had the sort of pointed hardness that came from an excess of pushups every morning. Far less interesting than 'Mina's, but impressive nonetheless.

Javier knew the woman had body issues. Nobody else would understand, looking at her, except by the implication of how hard she worked, every day, to look like that. But she would also do nearly as good a job of distraction in this situation as Wilhelmina would have.

There just weren't that many women, nearly that impressive, anywhere in the galaxy.

Javier wore an identical cloth, clipped on his left. He generally worked out, and was in good shape for a spacer in his early forties, but nobody was in Sykora's league. Plus he was as hairy on legs and arms and chest as she was smooth.

At least none of it had started turning gray yet.

She studied him with a look of bored contempt that she must have learned from 'Mina, back when she was learning to walk sexy from the smaller woman. Javier grinned pure insolence up at her, and then nodded for her to precede him.

Out in the hallways, it was indeed early in the local day, probably set to *Altai's* capital city. Locals were probably fast a-bed now, as the only people they saw while they walked wore the tan slacks and green shirts of staff, brightly different from the hard gray of technical crew.

They turned a corner after a few minutes, and passed through another over-scale airlock into something approximating a locker room, with restrooms, showers, and more helpful staff on hand.

Another, smaller airlock, beyond that, and Javier had warm sand in his toes, sun just rising in what was now officially east, and a morning breeze crossing from left to right. Waves, not ten meters away.

And not one, damned seagull to be found, anywhere.

"What's that?" a voice jarred him out of his happy spot.

Her voice. Sykora.

At least it was curiosity and not pique. At least as near as he could tell.

A giant tree branch suddenly stretched out over his shoulder and in front of him. It took a moment to identify her arm as such. She was pointing at the spot in the middle of the room.

A monumentally large room.

"Shangri-La," he replied. "Private island for by-invitation-only guests and very private parties. Not anyplace I want to go. You neither."

"Huh," she replied noncommittal. "It would be an easy swim."

"Sure," he said. "Six hundred meters from here. Less if you catch the short axis. I'm not that ambitious to get thrown off the ship that quickly."

"Okay, then now what?" she asked.

Javier ignored the woman and walked twenty or forty meters to one side, crossing a few dunes and some sedge grass until he found the right spot, not too far from the water, slightly private as dunes created a small amphitheater effect.

Perfect.

Javier unclipped his towel, stretched it out, and laid down to catch some of the early morning sun. He might be naturally much darker than Sykora, but his tan still needed work.

"Hey, what do I do?" she asked again as he closed his eyes.

Javier opened them again. From here, she was a kilometer tall.

"Bodyguard," he replied. "If you think a mermaid might get me. Tan, maybe. Nap? Or swim some. Up to you."

She glared prodigiously down at him, again Athena atop Olympus. For a moment, he thought the Dragoon might seriously go tactical on an empty beach, but she dropped her towel next to him, jutted a chin rudely in his direction, and raced out into the surf.

Aphrodite in reverse, disappearing under the waves.

"So," a new voice intruded on his consciousness after a few moments. "Should I read that as faith in the competence of my staff? Or insolence, on the part of yours?"

Javier's eyes snapped open to find a woman standing suddenly on his other side, grinning lightly at him.

Like Sykora, the stranger had worn only a wrap this morning. She wasn't as hardbody as the Dragoon, but that still left a lot of space for amazing, volume she filled like jasmine. Even 'Mina would have probably been a distant third.

Her skin wasn't as dark as Javier's, and it was a richer golden tone where his brownness tended towards ochre. Her hair was long and black, straight nearly down to her bottom. Pixyish green eyes.

Stunning. Utterly stunning.

And she knew it. Practiced it. Broadcast it on all channels.

"Both, Your Grace," Javier said evenly after a moment of appreciation.

He flipped a coin in his head and decided to remain horizontal, at least until she said something about it.

"You know who I am?" she inquired in a coquettish voice.

"I am staying in a guest room," he said. "Best to know who the host is."

"I see," she said.

She unhooked her wrap and laid it beside him, dropping down and folding herself into a perfect lotus, facing him from close enough he could feel the heat radiate off her knees, and smell the coconut oil she had rubbed on her legs in the last few hours.

"You are Navarre," she announced in a quiet, sure voice. "The pirate."

Javier knew a moment of pure panic.

That perhaps this beautiful woman had somehow been a friend of someone on Tamaz's crew. That he was a dead man, and had just found his executioner.

He studied her face sidelong, let his gaze drift and linger.

Black widow was another option.

Not necessarily the preferred outcome, but something about condemned men and last meals came to mind.

Navarre growled in his mind, so Javier let the man take over.

"And?" he rasped.

"Are you a killer, Navarre?" she asked. "Or merely a thief?"

"Or?" he asked back, rusty, jagged edges appearing in his voice.

He turned his head to face her more fully. She smiled wickedly.

"You left out gentleman, rogue, and card sharp," Javier said in a lighter tone, pushing the killer back into the shadows of his mind. "I also dance a pretty good Argentinian Tango."

"Do you now?" she pursued. "Tango? It can be hard around here, finding a man willing to force the rhythm, but comfortable letting a woman have the power to improvise. Who understands that there are lines that must be colored outside of, occasionally."

Javier smiled laconically and shrugged.

Black widow, indeed.

She leaned forward a bit. Not enough to block the pseudo-sun's light, but towering more over him now.

"Are you here to kill someone, Captain Navarre?" she purred.

Javier grinned up at her.

"No, actually," he confessed. "This is probably the one time where I get a vacation and nobody has to die."

"Has to?" she dripped verbal honey on his chest.

"There are always bad seeds, *Khatum*," he felt his smile grow harder. "Back home, we called it the *Texas* defense. As in: *Yer Honor, he needed killin'.*"

"Like Abraam Tamaz?" she asked.

Yup. A reputation could be a good thing, or a bad thing, but it was still a thing.

"There are few people more deserving," Javier said with a hard smile. "Somebody had to do it."

"So you are the kind of man who takes charge, when he sees something that needs doing?" she asked lightly. "Grabs life by the hair and pulls?"

"Never without an invitation," he replied laconically.

Somehow, she was floating above him. Javier could only imagine the flexibility she must have, to remain in a full lotus and still be able to lean so far forward that they could start necking without him moving too much.

"I'll keep that in mind," she whispered.

Javier could smell the mouthwash she had gargled with this morning. Minty, but not overwhelming. His breath probably smelled like coffee, but that was the chance you took, hitting on strangers on a beach.

She glanced up suddenly and smiled at him with promise as she leaned back.

"Your bodyguard is getting nervous," she said, returning upright.

Javier watched her unhook her feet, wriggle a bit, and stand up in a single motion. Rather than hook the wrap about her hips, she tossed it over one forearm and began to walk away in such a direction that Javier had the best view of her bottom.

"We shall talk again, Captain Navarre," she called over one shoulder with a tinkling bell of a laugh as she disappeared over a dune.

"Sorry," Sykora observed from two meters away, without the least apology in her voice. "Didn't mean to interrupt the two of you rutting on the beach. Who was that?"

Javier turned his head the other direction, but not until the first woman was out of sight.

Sykora was dripping water into the sand. Cold water, from the tightness of her nipples, in spite of the warm breeze. Nude, just as the *Khatum* had been. Female, as well.

That was about where the comparisons ended.

No. Dangerous. Both of them.

Black widows. Just different kinds.

He hoped.

"The *Khatum of Altai*," he said. "Our host."

"Wow, you work quickly," she sneered down at him from her majestic perch.

"She generally doesn't discriminate," he fired back. "Feel free."

Sykora rewarded him with a silent snarl.

The first time he had said something like that to the Dragoon, she had bounced him off a bulkhead hard enough to give him a concussion. She was either relaxing as she grew up, or taking her role as his bodyguard more seriously.

Javier reached out and patted her towel with a serious look. The kind that said: *Don't argue.*

She thought about it anyway for a moment. That much was obvious, but she stretched out her towel and sat.

Two lovers enjoying the beach. As if.

"We need to move quickly," Javier said simply. "Our cover can't stand the kind of inspection that woman might bring to bear."

"Not going to play with your new friend?" Sykora asked sweetly.

"Hadiiye," he said in a quiet, serious tone. "She's likely to just shoot us in the back of the head if she thinks we're a threat. No trial. No excuses. Nothing. She knows who I'm supposed to be, so we need to get gone."

That got through.

Death-machine there drew a quiet breath that suggested the scale of risk was finally coming home.

"What did you find in the vault?" the Ballerina of Death asked quietly, pivoting with all the mental prowess she brought to combat.

She might have been commenting on the surf for all the emotion in her voice.

"A woman who likes to brag," Javier replied sourly. "Vanity and ego undo so many morons. But I never saw the vault itself. Handed over the box to a guard, got a receipt when it was delivered."

It was necessary to peek over his shoulder, like this was a bad holo, but he couldn't help himself.

Nobody was sneaking up on them. No arresting angels swooping in.

"Very few guests actually live here," he continued. "And those that do don't bring huge amounts of jewelry with them. There are way more interesting resorts at which to get dressed up and hit the casinos."

"So?"

Now Sykora had managed to sound bored. Obviously, another talent she was perfecting as she became an actor.

"So thirty-six boxes in one wall," he replied. "Different heights, escalating widths. Our helmet went into the fifth row, bottom spot, to give you an idea."

"And we know one of them holds our box?" she asked, ever so slightly interested now.

"We presume," he replied. "She had to brag that their security was good enough for visiting royalty. Present tense, not past. If I can get the probe in there through the air vents, we should be able to scan it and know how to get in."

"And then what?" Sykora asked.

Her voice was starting to edge into that place Javier liked to think of as High Priestess of the Goddess of Death. The amazing, lethal creature that had come to the fore when they were escaping *Salekhard*.

"Navarre was probably hired because someone wanted a mass casualty incident," Javier sneered at her. "Most of the ways to access that vault require a distraction of a scale that someone gets killed, even accidentally."

"So?"

"So I want a reputation as more than just a killer, Hadiiye," he retorted. "It opens us up to more opportunities, better jobs. That much faster I can pay you and Sokolov off and get on with my life."

"One of us probably still has to die first," she whispered fiercely.

"Maybe," he agreed. "But not today. Okay?"

Javier could see her weigh the alternatives. He probably looked like that around her, from time to time, because, yeah, one of them probably would have to die, but they could still be professionals about things until then.

She nodded, implicit with the sort of emotion and violence that drove Shakespeare to greatness.

"What's the immediate plan?"

"Back to the room in a while," he stated. "We'll have a good meal, and then beg off everything and everyone with a serious case of starship lag. I'll go to bed, as it were, to catch up on my sleep. You'll go seduce a crewmember."

"Seduce?" she snarled in a whisper. "Fornicate?"

"If that's what it takes, yes."

Javier felt his voice go cold and lethal.

"Anything less than that is also acceptable, as long as you get me the answers and gear we need to pull this off."

"Bastard," she hissed.

"Princess, you have no idea."

# PART FIVE

Suvi took a moment to consider the right music for this sort of mission. In all the videos, the hero always flew into battle with some serious backbeat drums over a screaming string section, either an electric guitar or a full orchestra.

But she was really more of a cat burglar today, instead of potentially flying a hard strafing run in a tight canyon.

In the end, she settled for Rachmaninoff's Third Piano Concerto. Music for someone born without fear. Just for fun, she spun up a couple of jazz improvisation sub-routines for drums and bass, then let them duel elegantly with the piano as she moved.

The Dragoon had disappeared after the two of them had come back from dinner, leaving her and Javier alone to talk shop for several hours while he added a small electric screwdriver with a rotating multi-head to her outer shell.

Finally, *hands*. She was going to insist he add something at least as good to the big ship when they got home, plus a bigger waldo or something so she could manipulate things.

There was nothing as annoying as having to bonk your nose on a door chime to get it to ring.

And now, the thief in the night.

Someone had given a lot of thought to the architecture of this resort. The square air vent she was cruising down was forty centimeters tall and fifty wide. Too small for most humans, and too dusty for her to worry about running into a cleaning robot.

Not that she was really concerned about running into a drone, except that it might think she was a rodent or something. After all, what self-respecting AI would be happy as a maid-drone?

Nope. Flittering along, happily listening to one of the most dangerous men ever allowed to touch a piano. No annoying Red Baron. Nothing.

Just Suvi, dressed in a skin-tight, black, leather body suit. The kind without any seams at all, and nothing riding up uncomfortably as you moved.

You could do that when you were an AI.

She had kept the scanner pings down to nearly nothing, relying on Visual Flight Rules and passive sensors for now. There was enough light coming in from the regular vents that her optical sensors were fine.

A girl just had to peek and sneak past them, only committing a little voyeurism as she did.

Humans, for all their diversity, tended to be pretty predictable, but she wasn't really interested in expanding her horizons of experience today.

According to inertial guidance and some math, she should be getting close. Just around a corner and…

*Yup. Paranoia.*

Someone had hung a *something* there, right across the duct.

A human would have probably missed it, relying on eyes, but Suvi at least had been listening with all her extra senses. It was a field of some sort, but not a defensive grid.

She moved just close enough that an arcshield would have sparkled as a warning before it zapped her.

Nothing.

And she realized that everything beyond it was invisible on every wavelength except visual.

*Huh. Somebody had a clue. Not a full one, but a clue.*

Suvi hovered low enough to look at the emitters on top. She was pretty sure it was a simple electromagnetic shield, designed to prevent someone like Javier from flying a remote control drone in here, exactly like she was doing.

After all, who would pour a full AI into something so petite?

*Okay, truth or dare time.*

Suvi landed with a soft kiss, back about a meter. If this was really just a shield, she would lose most of her systems passing through, and have to reboot everything. A dumbbot could go autonomous on the other side, but that was exactly where you needed smarts.

She rolled herself forward like a marble, all the way through the field.

*Oh, that tickles.*

*And darkness.*

Suvi took a deep breath and climbed under her flight console to crack open the breaker box. Most of the switches had tripped, just as she expected.

She took a few seconds to rocker each one back on line, rather than just pushing the reset button.

*Make it all good now, rather than miss something having issues later.*

She peeked at the next air vent. It looked right. Big lobby with red sofas and stuff, just like Javier had described it.

And empty. Height of the party time. Everyone should be at the luau chomping down on fresh-cooked pig.

She took the next left and looked down from her parapet.

One guard. Headphones plugged in. Scanning a dozen monitors and a mixing board-worth of gauges.

And bored.

*If he were panicking, he would have slammed shut the air vent, just in case, and be pushing buttons frantically. I'm just a mouse in the cupboard.*

Suvi skittered past and found the room she wanted next. Empty.

The Vault. Long wall of cubicles you could shut, with curtains over there. Couple of comfy chairs. Seriously secured door. Wall of box-drawer-thingees full-o-stuff.

This was where it had gotten iffy. Javier had thought everything would work, but he wasn't four meters tall and couldn't just climb up here and make sure she could get the angle she needed.

It was going to be close.

*Highest leftest. Maybe. Hung up on something. Oh, screw coming through the metal grate. Can't move it out of the way. Drop down, twist a little, bip back up. There.*

Suvi took another deep breath, concentrating on her yoga sub-routines.

*Oh, what the hell.*

She cranked Sergei up loud enough she was pretty sure someone on the outside might see the shell physically vibrate.

She painted the room with a hard sensor pulse. A human might have actually felt that one, as the iron in their blood rotated for a microsecond. Then she spent nearly ten seconds doing signal processing, washing out noise.

Talk about an eternity.

Let's see. Jewelry. Jewelry. Gun. Gold brick? Really? Hey, there's the helmet. Jewelry.

They had three potential targets when she was done. And four on the far right she had been unable to scan from here.

*And seriously, who the hell used mechanical keys anymore? One kiss from a computer and you could open any of them.*

*Oh, right. Any of them. Yeah, no. Key actually made more sense. You could still pick it or masterkey it if you had to, but nobody could upload an AI into the system and just trigger all the doors and stuff.*

Suvi backed out of her corner and began to backtrack, careful to peek at the one guard, but he was still sitting pretty and occasionally flipping a button.

*Pretty sneaky, lady. I'll give you that. Ya went old school on me. Keys. But I can take you.*

# BOOK ELEVEN: BLACK WIDOWS

PART ONE

Javier poured himself a highball glass of real Earth Scotch and added two cubes of ice, swirling the liquid just enough to start that magical, chemical reaction to turn paint thinner into caramelized smoke. He flipped on some modern dance pop synth and dialed it down to ambient noise.

Just enough.

He was just about to get stretched out and put his feet up when the door chime ran through the Westminster sequence politely.

Nothing good would come of it.

Sykora was off grinding her teeth and possibly shaking her ass. Probably in that order.

Suvi should be about a third of the way into the hoard of the dragon by now.

There was nobody else on this ship he wanted to talk to.

The chime rang again, insistent.

Javier sighed, already regretting.

"Room system," he said in a dreary voice. "Activate hall monitor."

The wall in front of him lit up with a slightly fish-eyed view of the corridor outside.

And a black widow.

She might be one of the most beautiful women he had ever met, but Javier had no doubt that the *Khatum of Altai* wasn't here for intellectual stimulation.

No, he was most likely just the latest flavor of the week. Bored, rich aristocrats needed constant stimulation and degeneration.

Someone had once suggested that the alternative was actually turning their brains on and thinking, but too many would commit suicide, once they realized how dull and pointless their lives were. Usually, they just burned out on chemicals, ever-escalating the dosage, never addressing the underlying hollowness.

Javier had two ex-wives. And a former naval career. He understood that part.

At least he had gotten over himself, eventually.

"Room system, activate comm," he continued. "Good evening, madame. I will be right there."

Javier cut the audio and sipped a good hit of whiskey as he rose.

In for a penny, in for a pound.

The air vent cover was askew enough to let Suvi roam. Javier reached up and hung it back in place, pushing the screws into a handy drawer for now. Suvi had enough juice for weeks, and enough movies and books for at least one night.

He opened the door to his doom.

Whatever *it* was, she had it in spades.

Her smell embraced him as soon as the door opened. Light and sweet and flowery. The subtlest hint of just-blooming roses.

She wore black, possibly shrink-wrapped on, with panels cut out that just showed off the healthy glow of her golden skin and emphasized the curves and lines. He had already seen it all, but this just tantalized as a reminder that he had never touched.

Someone had braided her ebony hair up into a sort of mohawk, a blacktip shark's fin set to slice the water as she attacked. She was already tall for a woman. This put the top of her hair even with the top of his head.

Subtle, but effective.

Predator.

Black widow.

And she was alone.

"I wanted to make sure you were well," she murmured, stepping close enough to rest a palm on his chest. "They said you had an early dinner and then retired. And gave your Amazon the night off."

"Time synch issues," Javier lied blandly. "I was just having whiskey. Nightcap?"

Distracted women are less dangerous than thwarted ones. Bored girls like bad boys. Dilettantes didn't even notice science nerds.

"Please."

She smiled with perfect, gleaming teeth. Javier stepped back and to the side as she entered.

"So you're safe here?" she asked, walking over to the wetbar expectantly.

Javier took his cue and materialized a second glass from underneath. He let his back-brain work while he ogled the woman.

"I'm not expecting an assassin," he retorted wryly. "One is never sure about *safe*."

"Your Amazon is off enjoying herself," the woman purred.

"She only keeps me alive because she wants to kill me herself," Javier smiled.

It was the honest truth. Probably the only truth that would see the light of day on this mission.

He handed her the glass by stepping too close.

"You know how dangerous some women can get," he said.

He had to give her credit. The head tilt was perfect. The coy, coquettish giggle that escaped her lips could have won awards.

Her smell was desire itself.

"And Navarre isn't dangerous?" she whispered.

Javier leaned even closer. Not as a prelude to a kiss, but just to get almost nose to nose with this woman.

"Navarre will do absolutely *anything* to win."

Javier left just enough burr, just enough rusty razor blade in his tones, that the *Khatum*'s pupils dilated unconsciously.

Bored aristocrats. Even black widows.

Think they're tough. Have no clue what dangerous really looks like, cocooned warmly in the swaddling clothes of money.

His eyes sneered at her and her money. At her power. Even her perfection.

Navarre would kill her just as simply, just as easily, as he had Abraam Tamaz, if push truly came to shove.

"Anything?"

Her musk was palpable.

Javier rated himself about a nine for the performance. Some nights, the stars just aligned. He'd won a good chunk of the down-payment for *Mielikki* on *Merankorr*, on a night like that.

Javier leaned back a shade. His glass was still sitting on the end table, forlorn and forgotten.

"Everything."

Rough hands took her by the shoulders and turned her enough that his chest was suddenly pressed against her back, leaving his hands free to roam over the black silk, exploring the woman's perfection encased underneath.

He wasn't a priest, or a Speaker of the Word. Sin in his definition involved denying one's self the simple joys in life, like a beautiful woman demanding physical satisfaction.

There was nothing he could do about the ugliness that was her soul.

Maybe he'd have to send 'Mina here someday, to preach.

The *Khatum* leaned back heavily into him, purring, but otherwise still. He didn't figure that would last long, not with a woman like this. But he wasn't expecting either of the girls back anytime soon.

So he grabbed her by that lustrous, black hair, tugging it, just as bit, as he moved it to the side and nibbled on the woman's neck.

It would be in character, for a man like Navarre.

Just one of the sacrifices he was willing to make.

PART TWO

SHE KNEW she was in the right place by the lack of noise.

It wasn't one of the dance clubs that Djamila found herself in tonight. No, this had the feel of a neighborhood dive, that corner bar back home where most of the seats at the bar were specifically reserved by name and time, for the locals who would come in at the end of their day. That long, glass-mirrored, back bar, stacked with exotic bottles that would be refilled from industrial drums. The bald, heavy-set Publican in the stained apron, the kind with a gruff word and a scarred ear.

Djamila might have called it home.

Aritza had always been an officer. Had never served on the lower decks. Never answered beck and call. Might know places like this, but had never belonged to one for longer than his credit or his leave time.

The shifts on a ship in space would be constant. The clientele would turn over smoothly, without surging up and down as daylight came and went. Most of the people in here wore gray, although there were a few Staff in brighter colors. Those looked the surliest. Probably with reason.

Djamila pointed at the bar and then silently drew her hand to the left to indicate every stool. Most of them were empty, right now.

The Publican nodded in response, moving to one end of the bar and setting down an empty glass for her.

Djamila followed and climbed onto the stool.

She was supposed to be acting right now. Scouting. Seducing.

First, she needed a drink. Something that would provide a layer of insulation, demarcation, separation between who she was, and what she had to do tonight.

She already owed Aritza. Now she was keeping score.

The bartender held a bottle ready.

She nodded, digging out a couple of coins and a tip. He had already earned it, as far as she was concerned, just accepting her here. She was an outsider.

Always pay attention to the invisible people. They're the ones that make your life better or worse, regardless of your intent and actions.

The pour was blue. A subtle, bartender joke that actually brought a smile to her face, as hard and sour as it had been.

He grinned back, nodded that she knew what to ask for, and wandered to the other end of the bar, polishing a clean glass and surveying his bar like a bear roused mid-winter.

The liquor was potent enough that she could nearly taste the raw alcohol from here. She wondered if it was the man's own slash, a recipe distilled down from generations of barkeepers. Designed originally to strip grease off industrial equipment.

She sipped.

Potent. Almost undiluted acid as it went down.

It was right at home with Djamila tonight.

Another sip, and the heat began to fortify her. Perhaps

power a transformation of a Dragoon into a bimbo secret agent.

That appeared to be Aritza's secret. Become someone else and everything you did left with them when you took the costume off.

If he could do it, she could. Would.

*Anything you can do, asshole.*

Djamila felt her shoulders come down. For a moment, she considered pressing the warm glass up against her forehead, to see if she could absorb the potency of the fluid that way. Then she realized that the role she was playing tonight allowed it.

She did.

It might have worked.

"That bad, huh?" a voice asked quietly.

Djamila's eyes snapped open, hands ready to lash out and shatter the glass into someone's face and then beat them to death.

Self-defense. The oldest law in the universe.

She had placed the man mentally when she sat down, but otherwise ignored him as a prop on her stage, occupying the middle of three stools on the short end of the bar, when she was on the last chair on the long axis. An empty stool separated them.

And light centuries.

Light skin, almost pale compared to her tan, or Aritza's natural brown. Short hair, dark enough under the dim quietness of the bar. The face looked forty. The eyes suggested four hundred.

If she radiated menace, he had all the emotional signature of a stone headland thrust into the face of the oncoming storm.

He wore gray. She remembered her mission. Even let a little truth out.

Those make the best lies.

"I would really like to kill someone, right now," she drawled in a voice made up of all of her day.

"I could tell that," he replied easily. "But you aren't from around here."

"And *he* would never be caught dead in a place like this," she hissed. "Not money enough, unless he's slumming."

The stranger gave her an appraising look. Not sexual, but interested in her story.

Djamila had worn blue dungarees and a black tunic. It stood out against all the charcoal gray in here, but not much.

He was a bantam. That was the only word she could think of to describe the man. She had at least half a meter in height on the man, she guessed, and probably thirty kilos of mass.

She took another sip of angry courage and let the fire stoke her *transformation*.

"Bodyguard?" the man hazarded a guess.

Djamila shrugged.

"Lethal moll, at least," she growled.

It was easier playing a part when you weren't playing.

"Yeah, I got the lethal part," he agreed. "Long day with a moron boss who won't listen?"

Djamila nodded.

No. *Hadiiye*. This was a role. She was an actress. They were on stage.

Hadiiye fixed the man with a hard stare. Challenging his right to speak with her.

And then she softened it. Her purpose here required communication. She couldn't lose track of that part.

"Dumbass with more muscle than brains," she agreed. "Luck and timing are the only things that have kept him alive this long."

"There are always other jobs out there, you know," he replied in a quieter voice.

Whispering to a wild animal, perhaps.

Violence wasn't far from her surface right now.

But not against this man.

Navarre. Aritza. Whoever he was.

And Sokolov, for even suggesting to her that Sascha or Hajna could have handled this job better than she could.

Someone else to keep score against. To prove wrong.

"Violence seems to be the only thing people think I'm capable of," Hadiiye retorted.

"It has its place," the little man agreed. "Some of us even get paid well and treated respectably for it."

Her eyes narrowed and she studied the stranger closer.

Perfect stillness. Something learned, not a natural trait in anyone.

Callouses on his hands from striking things repeatedly in training. Like her own.

More dangerous than he had first seemed.

Or perhaps he had been masking that before. Actors, on a stage.

"Bouncer?" she guessed.

He shrugged with petite eloquence.

"They have a more polite title for it aboard ship," he said. "But you are essentially accurate."

"Gray?" she asked.

"Staff-side are the friendly ones in bright colors," he smiled. "Ship-side wear gray. Makes us invisible. Until we need to not be."

She considered the man. The implications. The danger.

The reward.

"Ever hire Amazons?" she hesitated. "Almost anything would be better than the asshole I'm working for right now."

A hard gleam appeared in his eyes.

"Stand up," he commanded in a light tone. "Turn around."

She did, channeling everything Dr. Teague had ever taught her about Hadiiye.

The man's eyes on her body were like fingers, exploring, probing.

Caressing her skin.

She faced him again.

"Can you contain the violence?" he asked.

Hadiiye felt a thrill spike her.

Aritza considered her nothing more than a gun-bunny. Point and shoot.

This stranger understood that violence was only half of the training. Controlling it was almost more effort than unleashing it. And more important.

"With my size, menace is almost more useful," Hadiiye replied. "Most of the time."

"How many people have you killed?" he asked. "Personally."

"When I was a soldier? Hundreds, perhaps thousands," she said. "Since then, dozens. Maybe scores. I don't really obsess or keep score."

"You might look good in gray," he hazarded.

"Ha. You haven't even got a uniform that would fit me," she spiked him with her eyes.

Challenge.

Not menace. Dare.

His eyes got cagey.

Challenge accepted.

"If you have an hour, we could try sneaking into the quartermaster section and stealing you something," he said, eyes lit with a mischievous fire.

She had learned the right way to arch an eyebrow from

Dr. Teague. Compelling disbelief conveyed, without sarcasm or sound.

"Sounds like an excuse to get me someplace private and take advantage of me," Hadiiye purred.

Not quite an invitation. Maybe.

The mission.

Again, his eyes roamed. Scales in his head weighed options.

"Maybe," he said. "A little."

He held out a hand.

"Farouz," he introduced himself.

"Hadiiye," she took his hand. "I don't normally let strangers seduce me in bars, you know."

"That's because you intimidate the hell out of most people," he replied.

"Most?"

"Most," he grinned, sliding off the stool.

She joined him.

One hundred sixty-five centimeters tall. Maybe. Wiry and hard.

His eyes were about on a level with her nipples.

Probably a good thing that dancing wasn't on the menu.

Presently.

She joined him, a tree next to a rosebush.

"Lead on," she said.

This was when it was going to get interesting.

# PART THREE

Javier felt like ten kilometers of bad, gravel road.

Heaven forbid that if he ever decided to take up running marathons, he would probably feel like this for the first six months. Which would be the point he gave up and went back to less strenuous pursuits.

The *Khatum* didn't snore, but she was purring, fast asleep on a cream, silk-covered bed that looked like a mugging. The chair by the door was in worse shape, with all their clothes thrown at it as they went by. Destructive whirlwind kind of night.

For a woman with four grown children, a topic he had researched before arriving, she still looked and acted like she was thirty-two standard. And possibly a nymphomaniac at that.

Or just bored with all the fashion-model aristocrats and boy-toys around here. Not much had changed.

If he was planning to stay long, she'd probably work him to death.

But that wasn't going to be a problem. The only risk was

dying if she caught his lies, or decided to send ninjas after him later.

At least the bed was big enough he could stretch out on his side and leave three quarters of it for her. He pulled a couple of pillows up and leaned back, sipping a glass of water from the table. It wouldn't do to fall asleep with this woman here. Not with the other two women due back at some point.

At the same time, he couldn't go anywhere.

Javier could just see Suvi's flitter returning, and him pulling the grate open for her, right as the *Khatum* staggered from the bedroom looking for him.

Talk about lethally awkward.

Sykora wouldn't be as bad, but there was always a chance her mission would end up requiring her to bring a guy back here. He really didn't want to end up being her dad, tonight.

The purring stopped.

She stretched in place for a moment, athletic beauty a distraction all by itself, and then rolled over to look at him.

"That could be addicting," she murmured. "It's a good thing you're only passing through."

Navarre's cold mask studied the woman before it relented into something like a smile.

"Oh?" he asked.

"Some people are obsessed with wealth and power," she said, pulling the silk sheets up to make a little cocoon fortress around herself. "They sniff around and try to worm their way in. Those I've already defeated."

"Did you now?" he asked in a soft, lyrical tone. "How?"

"When I became the heir, I changed the rules," she said. "Any man wanting me was required to make a set of deposits in a sperm bank ahead of time. I left them there for five years and let the men make their case."

"And how did that turn out?" Javier asked.

This was certainly a novel way to handle men, and probably a pretty effective method.

"When I was ready, I used those samples to impregnate myself," she smiled cruelly. "None of the men was told who, and they all looked close enough alike. I ended up with boy/girl fraternal twins on the second round, and now I have four children, with twelve fathers. One of the children will become the heir, and the other three will be married off well."

"And did it succeed?" Javier asked, rolling a little onto his side to focus more of his attention on her. She felt vulnerable right now.

It might be an act. It might be a trap. It might be an opportunity. And maybe she was hungry for a second round or a second dinner.

Javier's only mission right now was distraction. And she made that such a chore. Honest.

"Boring," the woman sulked a bit. "Beautiful songbird. Golden cage. A story as old as time and money."

She shrugged with her whole body, stretching the semi-translucent silk tight to distract him. It worked.

"And I'm just another bad boy?" Javier teased.

"Worse," she replied. "A consummate professional with a goal. I just happen to be a pleasant diversion. If I hadn't come along, you might have listened to opera all night instead, wouldn't you?"

"*Cyranean* Pulse," Javier replied. "But yes, you are essentially correct, *Khatum of Altai*."

"I have a name," she snapped.

"And we have not been formally introduced, madam," Navarre's voice whip-cracked back at her.

He waved at the remains of the bed.

"Though this hardly qualifies as a formal salon against

which we could explore the social geometries of Kierkegaard," he continued in a cruel voice.

She shifted herself around, almost angrily, until she was also upright, with a pillow behind her and those distracting golden-brown breasts resting on a sea of ecru silk. Her eyes were fire.

And then they sparkled.

"No, I suppose not," she said with a sudden, bright giggle, also waving at the destroyed bedding. "But our activities here would either constitute a concrete refutation of existentialism, or its logical conclusion. Two strangers seeking meaningless pleasure in one another. I suppose one's take on the balance between Deism and Romanticism would determine which side of the coin landed upright, wouldn't you agree? And you may call me Behnam, at least in private."

For a moment, Javier knew pure lust.

All that, and brains, plus an amazingly rare level of education. Certainly not the sort of woman to take home to meet his parents, but *wow*.

"My mother named me Eutrupio," Javier said.

And it wasn't even a lie.

Javier Eutrupio Aritza. Or Eutrupio Navarre, he supposed, if one wanted to be philosophical.

Navarre would never admit to softer emotions or philosophical permutations, but he was a boring shit. Too linear.

"If the Creator actually cares," Javier opined, waving a hand at the room, "then we're probably all going to hell. Perhaps we did and just haven't been judged wanting. At least not yet."

"Who are you, Navarre-the-killer?" she asked, leaning towards him.

"A man making his way best he can," Javier replied with a

shrug. "There are amazing distractions, if one stops to smell the roses."

"And you'll be here an entire month?" she asked breathlessly. "On someone else's credit?"

"That's the current plan," he lied breezily. "It will depend on the buyer's ability to get here."

She rolled away from him and stood up on her side of the bed.

"In that case," she said, sashaying towards the pile of clothing. "Next time, I might let you scrub my back. But we should save some things. Wouldn't want to show you everything all at once."

Javier let himself stare lustfully at the woman. It was rude, and she seemed to thrill in it, stretching the black fabric around her in ways that made her body even more interesting than it was nude. There was nothing to do about the remains of her mohawk braid, except pull it all back and strut home.

Oh, the hard life of a space pirate.

"Will you be recovered enough to join us for an event tonight?" Behnam, the *Khatum of Altai*, asked lightly. "Or should we give you another day?"

Javier shrugged. Navarre was a bad-ass who would admit no fear, no exhaustion. Nothing.

And boring as shit.

"I'm still star-lagged," he replied. "Someone interrupted what would have been a solid night of meditation and sleep, so I would vote for another day of rest, if I need to show up all the locals."

She grinned back at him and subtly transformed back out of that vulnerable girl she had been and into the hard-ass businesswoman who was one of the richest people in the sector, and one of the most dangerous.

"Then you will most definitely need your rest, Navarre,"

she smiled cruelly. "There are many who will want to take your measure."

Without another word, she turned and left.

Javier let her go. There was nothing to be gained by trying to get in a last word, not now.

Because there was no way in hell he was going to be here in two days to say it.

DJAMILA WATCHED Farouz peek out the door one last time and then close it in silence. She found herself leaned back against a shelving unit taller than she was. The whole room was an oversized closet, maybe four meters by six, with clothing neatly folded and stacked by size. All of it gray.

He turned back and smiled up at her.

"So far, so good," he said in a voice barely above a whisper.

They had stealthily made their way back down a series of otherwise hidden hallways, accessible from the main part of the ship in many places, but separate from the world of wealth and dissipation outside.

"Why mechanical locks everywhere?" she asked, more curious than anything. "And where did you learn to pick them?"

He shrugged and stepped away from the door. Not close, but closer.

"We get a number of really smart people here," he said. "Bankers and finance people. Good with computers. Got to be too much hassle to keep them from damaging systems trying to override them. Mechanical locks are so old-school that you have to study them in order to get by. And develop a very soft touch."

"Soft?" she asked.

Farouz took another partial step closer.

"Just so," he agreed. "Light enough to find the right spot. Firm enough to tease it into position. Strong enough to hold it perfectly still, while everything else moves for you."

"We're still talking about locks?" she teased.

"Everything is secured," Farouz grinned. "Getting it open so you can access something takes time and patience."

He was suddenly close. Arm's reach for him with shorter arms. His eyes had a gleam in them Djamila wasn't sure she'd ever seen before.

Desire.

Not lust. Not power. Not control.

Want.

It was alien to the Ballerina of Death, but not necessarily unwelcome.

"So did you bring me here to seduce me?" she whispered. "Or show off your lock-picking skills?"

"There's a difference?" he whispered back, staring up at her from breathing range.

"Yes," she said. "You still haven't shown me anything in gray that would convince me this is the kind of place I might fit."

"Fit is important," he agreed. "We should find you something that fits just right. Fills that burning need."

Djamila suddenly felt fifteen again, on the verge of losing her virginity to a fellow student. It hadn't been that great, nor had others, but the edge of excitement and danger was there.

She smiled. Considered kissing the man. And not kissing him. Danced wickedly outside of herself.

Farouz took a step back and studied her in slow detail. His hands flexed like he wanted to use his fingers to measure her and not just his eyes.

"It helps that you are proportioned more like a man," he said. "I can only imagine the impossibility of finding pants if you were all leg."

He turned to his left and studied the shelves.

Djamila let out a silent breath. So close. And so strange.

When was the last time she had felt desire?

Farouz kneeled down and pulled a bundle from a bottom shelf, unfurling it and holding it up to her hip.

"Perhaps a single roll at the hem, until you sew it under," he said with a leering smile. "Jacket will be easier."

A moment or two later, he handed her a shirt and a jacket from another shelf.

"Try this on," he said, moving to the door and turning his back on her.

Djamila started to strip immediately, but Hadiiye stopped her.

"You aren't going to watch?" Hadiiye asked slowly.

"It might be considered rude," he said back over a shoulder. "Seeing things I wasn't supposed to."

"Supposed to?" she inquired with a saucy edge so unlike herself she nearly gasped. "I think you should see how everything fits. You brought me here, you know. You have some responsibilities for the fashion."

She watched him turn slowly back, facing her while leaning back on the door. She was expecting a leer, but got a warm smile instead.

Slippers off first, she pulled the tunic over her head. It was a thick fabric, and they were shipboard, so she had nothing under it but tan.

The slacks went next. Again, nothing but skin.

She lingered over the new t-shirt, putting it to one side

after a few beats so she could pick up the pants and slide them over her long, bronze legs, watching his eyes every step of the way.

He stared right back at her, eyes locked as she moved.

Farouz's eyes drifted when she pulled the shirt over her head and tucked it down tight against her skin.

She told herself it was cold in here.

The jacket was last, and then she stood before him transformed.

"How long is your moron boss going to be aboard?" Farouz asked in a breathless voice.

"We're scheduled for several weeks," Hadiiye purred back. "I'll have a lot of personal time available."

He stepped closer. Again, close enough to breathe on, but not touching her at all.

Pointedly so.

"I have to go on shift in an hour or so, and pull a double because Derek is on medlist," Farouz replied. "I would like to take you out to dinner in forty-eight hours, and then properly seduce you."

"And not now?" Djamila asked, breathless all of a sudden.

One of his hands went around her hip and pulled her close. She leaned down so they could kiss, but it was over almost immediately.

Djamila lurched, but only in her head.

"Cheap flings are just that," he murmured. "I'd rather show you a better side of the world."

He stepped back.

"Thank you for that, though," he said. "I could never have imagined something so amazing."

She let the thrill fill her. And relaxed.

"What about this?" she asked, starting to unbutton the jacket.

"Keep it," he said. "A crew this big will never notice, and if you wore it in two days. we could go nearly anywhere aboard ship and nobody would ask."

She smiled.

"It's a date."

# BOOK TWELVE: GRAY

PART ONE

JAVIER WAS TYPING into Suvi's communication keyboard rather than talking out loud, because he couldn't be sure how late Sykora would be out. The rest of the board didn't really do anything important, except play music, and make cute, little, furry animals dance across her dashboard. She did all the flying.

But it also irritated her to have to wait for him to type.

Javier suspected she was reading various books while she waited for him to use such a slow method of chatting. He considered flipping to an ancient Morse code keyboard to really slow things down, but she was already tart in her responses.

Not worth pushing it.

She was a good kid. With way more than she should. If not for him, she'd still be the monotonously-boring AI system that had come with his ship. Before he'd turned her into someone fun.

The outer door chimed once, and then opened.

Javier was in the main room. He wasn't sure if Sykora was

alone, or if he'd even see her tonight. Creator knew she was furious with him for assigning her that mission.

Her fault. Either of the pathfinder babes could have handled the job easier. Her professional pride would get her killed one of these days.

If this wasn't already such a dicey situation, he would have arranged for it to be sooner, rather than later.

And he had expected her to stomp into the room.

Instead, she entered like an ice skater, gliding effortlessly to a halt beside him.

Javier triple-taked and then nearly jumped out of the chair.

She was dressed in gray, holding a small bag of what he presumed were the clothes she had gone out in.

And she had a goofy grin on her face.

Man, this was probably worse than *Homicidal Amazon*.

She sniffed. Pointedly.

"Wow, you really do work fast," she announced in disbelief. "She's already been here, rolled you once, and left?"

"Sit," he commanded sourly. "We have to be done with this mission in twenty-six hours, then steal the cargo lighter and escape."

"Why?" she pushed back. "What's the rush?"

"You got a date or something?" Javier turned and looked up at her. Inspecting those little details.

Pupils dilated. Breathing shallow. Skin flushing suddenly. Jaw dropping open in shock.

Shit. She really did have a date. Her? Here? What the hell had she been up to, the last six hours?

Javier pointed at the sofa.

"Down," he commanded a second time. "If it's that important, we can always kidnap him at gunpoint later and take him with us."

Wow. Blush all the way down to her collar now. Like she was seriously considering it.

He watched her stumble to the sofa and collapse onto it.

"And I've never come home in someone else's clothes sober," Javier sneered at her. "So I'll assume you were successful. Spill."

Even more blush? How was that possible? And was she going to pass out shortly from all the blood flowing into her face?

It took a few seconds for her breath to get normal. And her usual anger to resurface.

The Ballerina of Death returned, took possession of the Dragoon. Good.

She was more predictable now. More professional. Possibly less dangerous.

"I made contact with a member of the security crew," she finally said, tones clipped sharp enough to shave on. "Allowed him to seduce me. Arranged a date for forty-six hours from now."

The blush returned, but nowhere near as bright.

"I was able to locate and acquire a uniform for myself," she gestured to those endless legs. "I can get you to the same location."

"Portal security?" he asked.

She was tactical now. He just needed to prod her in the right direction and duck, like pointing a cannon.

"There is a secondary set of corridors for Operations crew only," she responded. "Access is via a physical key turning counter-clockwise in a mechanical cylinder lock."

Damn, that was new. Or old, depending. And useful.

"How many keys did the man have?" Javier asked.

"Farouz only used one, that I saw," Sykora said, blushing some more.

Farouz, huh? Probably an ogre even taller than her. Must be a monster.

"How frequently were the corridors airlocked off?" he asked.

"Infrequent," she said. "And open, once we got into them. The only other time he needed to key a door was to get into the uniform closet."

Javier leaned back and thought. Suvi was listening, and could fill in all sorts of details later. From what he had already seen in the vault, getting into the boxes was also a mechanical process.

Everything was mechanical.

That was a maneuver so devious he could have never predicted it, but he had spent two hours in close contact with the mastermind behind it all. Nothing the *Khatum* did would surprise him.

Hopefully.

And hopefully, she wouldn't be terminally pissed at him when this was done.

He leaned forward and started typing into Suvi's keyboard.

Now was not the time to ask her to look something up for him. At least, not out loud.

The encyclopedia he had uploaded into her system was heavy on biology and applied sciences. It took up a tiny fraction of the space she had dedicated to books and movies.

Javier felt like a barbarian, working with stone knives and bear skins, to quote the ancient wisdom.

One article led to a second, a third, a fourth.

*Ah. There you are.*

The Science of Lock-picking. And the ancient tools of the trade. Something called a snap gun.

Insert a bar into the key slot. Turn the mechanism enough to just rub the pins inside and hold them tight. Tab them all upward simultaneously with a hinged pivot. Feel all the upper half of the pins come clear and release the lock. Turn the cylinder the rest of the way.

Billiards you played with small metal pins, using the same physics as an opening break.

Devious. Not a single i/o portal anywhere that he could plug Suvi into and let her tickle a computerized lock open, or beat the controlling software to death.

And he knew she had been so looking forward to it.

"I'll need access to a machine shop, or something similar," he said finally. "Twenty or thirty minutes and the right tools."

Sykora had been watching him, hawk-like.

He spun the display around for her to see.

"That's so ancient that I'm nearly offended," he continued. "But it's also genius. And easy enough for a competent systems tech to keep repaired. I had been planning to use software uploaded into the probe to defeat the door systems."

"And now?" she asked, breathless. "Are we blocked?"

The tone brought Javier's head up.

Was she looking for an excuse to get physical enough with this Farouz-fellow to lift his key? Sykora? The Ballerina of Death?

Officially weird. And yucky.

"No," Javier countered. "We sleep. We eat. We get ready. In about twenty-two hours we sneak out, do this thing, and then commit an act of piracy on the cargo lighter that will be docked and unloading. Those come in every twelve hours, so we should be good, if we can do everything else on time and get clear."

"And if not?" she asked.

"I'm sure the *Khatum* can find a yardarm to hang us from."

# PART TWO

Suvi had dialed the music down. Because now was most definitely not the time to get distracted by ten-finger, seventy-key piano solos.

A little Tchaikovsky for the booms, but mostly petite, chamber orchestras or octets. It fit with the gray uniform that Javier had stolen from the linen closet, itself a match with the one the Dragoon had apparently seduced her way into.

*Ew.*

Javier was carrying her right now in a fabric bag that barely blocked her visual sensors, to say nothing of everything else she had cranked up. Listening on just about every wavelength and pitch imaginable.

And he hadn't even had to let her hack into anything to steal the secret plans to this mammoth starship. Some fool had just left them on the entertainment system for the traveling engineer who was bored and wanted to see how the ship worked.

Suvi just knew that most people would never bother. Security by obscurity, after all, was as old as things to steal.

And even her digital scan of the locks in the vault wasn't

going to be all that helpful. Boss was going to go and invent himself an icepick, or a lockpick, or a stungun for lock systems.

Something.

She was too pissed at the whole situation to be rational at a time like this.

At least they had done a good job sneaking this far. But what fool put a simple air vent next to a secured door and expected everyone to miss it? Granted, Javier had, until she had highlighted it on the map and exploded it up as a full schematic with a small piano fanfare.

*I mean, hello?*

And Javier had finally stopped arguing with her and had let her hack the thing when they got there.

*Was that the right term? What do you call it when you fly up to a wall and unscrew the four bolts holding the damned screen in?*

*Stupid and amateur, that's what. Bad design engineering by a guy who really should have known better.*

And then back into the damned bag.

<grumblegrumblegrumble />

Suvi pinged an A-flat below middle C. Not too loud. Just enough to get Javier's attention.

And the psycho, paranoid floozy.

"What was that?" Sykora whispered in a tone shot through with adrenaline.

And craziness.

"Audio warning that we're approaching the machine shop," Javier murmured back in a tone right up there with soothing rabid Chihuahuas. "Remember, I programmed the probe to be much more autonomous than it used to be."

Or something like that.

*Whatever lies ya gotta tell these nutjob pirates until we can escape, boss.*

Javier's big mitt was warm as he reached into the bag, wrapping around her nude body like King Kong on a cold, Gotham night.

"Probe. Access Command Mode," Javier said formally, the phrase they had agreed to so she could pretend to be smarter than the waffle-maker. "Initiate security perimeter surveillance."

And then she was flying.

Free.

Well, stuck in a hallway that was dim by human standards and probably smelled weird, from the olfactory bio-readings she was tracking.

Good enough.

Suvi peeked once at the passive readings, and then booped the hallway with an ultrasonic pulse. Bats would be annoyed and bitchy right now, but nothing she had seen so far indicated sensors capable of detecting her call.

They were busy looking for radar and other silliness.

Nothing in the hallway either direction for a damned good distance. It was the middle of the night.

Next, she blasted the door with something kinda like X-rays, but not that far down the scale. Still let her see through walls.

Or would have.

Stupid bulkhead was apparently twice as thick as EVERY OTHER BULKHEAD ON THIS DAMNED SHIP.

*Fine.*

Suvi imagined big-girl panties she could pull up a notch, and then cranked the bass on her dashboard up to eleven.

<BONG />

*Oh, yeah. That's more like it.*

Apparently, nobody needed to secure the machine shop from vandals. And nobody was home.

She played a quick E-sharp/D trill. It sounded pleasant in

her ears. A quick spotlight nailed the door handle rather than the lock mechanism.

Javier grinned at her and nodded to the crazy woman.

He put a hand on the knob and twisted it open silently.

Inside was a paradise to make a girl engineer all tingly in the right places. Lathes, presses, laser beds. There was even a gas-flame welding bottle, for those times when you had to get all steel-welding and stuffff.

When using your own hands to do the job was going to be so much more satisfying than relying on mechanical assistance.

Suvi drifted into the room and took a deep sniff of heaven, the two humans trailing in her wake like amateur remorae.

Javier turned right immediately after closing and locking the door. Really thin bar stock was in a pigeonhole system, waiting for him like a poisoned princess.

Suvi was really pissed that the Dragoon was along.

There was no way in hell that Javier'd let her drive all these awesome machines, just like the girl back on *Storm Gauntlet* had gotten to make the helmet because there was no way to explain Javier programming the CNC machines to that level of pure awesomeness.

Still, he had promised her that the Dragoon was going to meet an unfortunate accident one of these days.

Suvi could wait.

PART THREE

It was one of the joys of a competent machine shop, Javier decided. And a well-organized one, as well. Everything was right where it was supposed to be.

The device he had thrown together was ugly. Rough. Crap, really, but it should do the trick. According to Suvi, they used a six-pin system here, with four heights programmable, or whatever the term was. Paranoid, compared to what was in the file, but not impossible.

Ninety-nine-point-something percent of the people that would pass through here would be stumped by all this. Of course, they hadn't been studying piracy with monomaniacal devotion for the last year, either. Javier did not appreciate what Sokolov and the Dragoon had turned him into, but he'd be utterly damned if he was going to do a half-assed job of it.

And now it was done. There was no locksmith shop in here for him to test against, but there were other ways.

"Get the door," he told Sykora as he moved that way.

She had been standing around, politely keeping her mouth shut for the fifteen minutes this took.

The woman just glowered at him.

"Please," Javier added.

Navarre never said please. Too much of him around lately. Even with Sykora.

"Probe. Access Command Mode," Javier called. "Scan the hallway when the door opens."

He waited.

The door opened on silent hinges, and nobody was standing there with a gun, waiting patiently.

So far. So good.

Suvi floated out, did her magic, and played him a happy trill.

Now the hard part.

Javier slid the thin metal bar into the lock awkwardly. Maybe some spray lubricant when they left? Something.

The theory was sound, but there'd been nothing to experiment on, and he knew it was all touch from what the files said.

Lock the latch from the back. Doorknob won't turn.

Damned barbarians and their lack of electronic keycards. At least the guest suites were civilized.

Jam it all the way in. Extra tap to be sure. Turn the metal until it stops moving. Hold firm.

Spin the little snapper thingee that was supposed to pop up all the pins at once.

Nothing.

Snap it again.

Hey, that was motion. Maybe half the pins?

"It's not working," Sykora said in a voice that somehow combined boredom with technical superiority.

"You don't get to use a crowbar to pry them open," Javier snarled quietly back. "And that would take a powered ram anyway. No way they wouldn't notice."

He turned back to the lock.

Snap it a third time, turning a little harder and the lock turned in his grip.

Stupid barbarians.

Okay, we can open locks. Painfully slow. Stupidly primitive. Brilliantly secure.

Bastards.

## PART FOUR

DJAMILA FELT HER HANDS TWITCH, fingers itching for a firearm. Something lethal to hold.

She had considered grabbing a piece of bar stock to carry, but that would be out of character for the crew. Ditto grinding an edge onto a piece of flat steel.

Besides, there was nothing here that would make her any more dangerous than her bare hands and feet, anyway.

Aritza's poisonous apple floated out ahead, high and up in the left-hand corner of the ceiling as they went. Humans tended to look up and left when they walked, so it might be invisible on their right.

Subtle things, but at least Aritza had programmed the device with some level of professional sense. Even if he never seemed to exhibit his own.

He had the controls now, but they were in his bag, and he was controlling the device with quiet, verbal commands. Again, an improvement. He could watch where he walked.

Djamila was torn on whether or not she missed the armed version that he had used to break her out of captivity.

Any gun handy would make her feel better. Even in his hands.

At least the hallway was empty.

She knew they were close, having memorized a variety of entry and exit paths.

The probe stopped over a closed door, dropped half a meter, and spun three-hundred-sixty degrees before bouncing back up to the ceiling.

She had been trailing Aritza. He glanced back at her and nodded.

The hallway was probably monitored by the man inside, if he was awake. The probe had carefully maneuvered to stay out of sight of the camera.

Djamila put on her acting persona and broadcast bored as she walked up and kind of stood next to the man.

Suspicious people act suspicious. She had just been called to duty to do something inane, when she could be out dancing. Djamila affected a slouch that wrapped her like a python, while maintaining a complete tactical perception field in three directions.

Child's play.

Aritza held a can of spray lubricant in one hand, and his lock-pick device in the other. A quick hiss, nearly inaudible, and then the whine of metal on metal.

Thrum-click.

Thrum-click.

Right about now, she came to know regret that she hadn't secreted a pry bar by her side as she walked. Something a meter and a half long, forged of hull metal, with a point on one end, and a wedge tip on the other.

Dumb-ass and his toy were going to fail. And the guard inside would wake up, panic, and trigger the alarm.

Djamila doubted they would hang.

The woman on the beach had looked like the kind to

walk them out an airlock with a view portal, and make a party of it, with champagne and finger food, while a string quartet played.

The kind of people who had made Djamila an outsider her entire life.

One might not choose to be a pirate, but one can make the most of it.

Thrum-click.

Third time apparently was lucky.

The handle turned.

The door opened inward.

Djamila already knew there was nobody in range, reinforced by the floating apple, so she stepped up and kicked the door with one, oversized, right foot.

It moved about fifty centimeters and bounced. Not enough to stop her mass. That was why she had used a foot and not a shoulder. More *oomph* behind it.

Someone inside had heard the noise and stood up to investigate. Djamila had just knocked him on his butt.

Another dumb-ass. He should have signaled an alarm of some sort first.

Maybe he had, and it just didn't sound in the hallway. Not her job, right now.

Djamila landed on the guy like a sack of potatoes as he struggled to get up.

Quick fist to the nose. Not enough to kill him. Just a stinger to blind and stun. An old fashioned crowd-control technique.

Open right palm to the cheekbone, backed by all her upper body. Again, not lethal. Just enough to rattle the brain around inside the skull. Mild concussion when done right.

Left hand, open palm. Snap him back the other direction.

*Good night.*

Djamila could almost feel the man's eyes roll back. He went limp under her.

She rolled him over onto his face, so he wouldn't choke on his tongue or anything, and checked over her shoulder.

Net time, less than two seconds.

Aritza and the probe were already inside the room, door closed and locked.

What idiot forgot to put a simple bar on this side, to keep people from doing exactly what they just had?

Oh, the arrogance of wealth.

Aritza pulled some ties from his bag, but Djamila had already found the cuffs the man kept in a pouch. She pulled both hands back, made sure everything was good, and snapped them into place.

She climbed off the poor man and moved around to check his pupils. Stunned and out cold, but nothing that a few hours of rest and some aspirin wouldn't cure.

A professional job.

She stood up.

The poor man even had a pistol in a holster he had never drawn. It was hers now. She attached it to her belt and drew the weapon.

Standard stun model. Short range. Good to take down nearly anyone, but not kill them, unless they suffered a stress-induced heart attack in the struggle. At which point, why the hell were they here instead of at a hospital getting that fixed up?

Aritza was already investigating the board with fingertips that never quite touched. He hummed quietly to himself as he did.

"Probe. Access Command Mode," he said, pulling a retractable cord from the console. "Standard i/o interlink available. Log in and review security systems."

The device dropped down and turned into a gray balloon floating above the console.

"Doesn't look like he sounded any alarms," Aritza continued, turning to her. "Did you check him for keys?"

Djamila blinked at him.

"Didn't think so," Javier said, kneeling down and grabbing a spool from the man's belt.

"This gets us halfway," he said as she continued to stare.

Djamila felt a blush come on. But she deserved this one. She had been unprofessional. Sure, take the man down rapid and silent. But she had gotten wrapped up in the gun and forgotten to check him for anything else.

She did now, but he had no radio tucked into a pocket, nor a knife. Nothing but pocket change.

Djamila stood, chastened.

And pissed.

Aritza kept making her look junior varsity, when she was the professional pirate.

She needed to up her game again. It was an arms race, now and forever.

"Halfway?" she asked.

"Every box has two keys," he said. "Guest has one. House has one. His. Now I only have to pick one lock each time."

Djamila nodded, looking down at the poor sap on the floor.

She had hoped otherwise, but her date with Farouz was definitely gone at this point.

Something else she owed Aritza.

# PART FIVE

Out of the security booth, down a short hall, and into the main vault Javier went, trailed by the two most important women in his life. Only one of them fell on the good side, but even the Amazon killer was important.

At least for now. Maybe she would suffer an accident at some point.

The risks of the profession.

The Vault hadn't changed in the last thirty-six hours.

On his right, a bank of cubby-holes for people to rest a box and sift through it behind a privacy curtain, as he had done before handing over the box and getting a key back. Several overstuffed chairs and a bench.

And paradise.

Six columns of lock-boxes. Six rows tall.

Farthest left were the narrowest at twenty centimeters wide. The top one was ten centimeters tall, and each of the five beneath it was five centimeters bigger as it went.

They got five centimeters wider with each column to the right.

Javier touched the bottom box on the fifth row, just for luck.

"This one is us," he said to the air.

Sykora just grunted back at him and moved to a spot where she could probably shoot anybody coming through either door into the place. She was like that.

Javier had already had a long conversation with Suvi, but he brought up the handheld anyway to be sure. Three distinct maybes. Four outside her scan range. Or had been, from the overhead air vent.

Not now.

"Probe. Access Command Mode," he called to her. "Hard scan the sixth column while I work."

He stuck the guard's master key into the lock. Or, tried to.

Wrong lock. Too wound up.

Deep breath. Calm. Professional.

Put it into the RIGHT lock and turn. Yes. There. Better.

Javier felt his whole being blip for a moment.

*What the hell?*

*Oh. Right. Hard scan. And that was just the back-scatter on her electromagnetic pulse? I wonder if we could turn it up and make a short-range weapon out of it, one of these days.*

*Remember to ask her. Or have her make a note to remind you.*

Something.

Javier sprayed the magic liquid into the first three locks Suvi had identified, and then put the bottle away for now.

Give it a moment to go to work.

Breathe.

He stuck the pick bar into One-Two and snapped the spinner. His own key to Five-Six only showed four teeth, so maybe this would be easier.

The lock turned. Either he was getting better at this, or he'd gotten lucky.

*And I'd rather be lucky than good.*

The outer face hinged open, revealing a fire-proof metal box.

He pulled it out, sat it on the floor and flipped it open.

Papers.

Deeds. Will. Identity papers from five different planets, in five different names, all with the same picture.

Stack of bearer bonds. Walk into any civilized bank and turn into money. Lots of money.

*How many zeroes?*

The evil conscience on his left shoulder giggled madly and then fell over dead as the good conscience on the right quick-drew a six gun and shot him.

"You don't even need to listen to that fool," the good angel said.

Javier agreed. None of this was what he wanted.

And if he took it, wouldn't that make him just another pirate? Like the crazy bitch behind him?

*No. Not going there. Not for you, lady. Not for anyone.*

He carefully restored it, closed the box, and stuffed it back into place.

The second box was harder to access. Five tries on the spinner before it bit.

Javier chalked that one up to nerves and adrenaline.

Inside was what appeared to be a manuscript. A big one. Printed on real paper. Hundreds of pages of what looked like some sort of lurid, historical romance, set in the Gas-Sailors Era of Old Earth, just before starflight.

Weird.

Javier had half a mind to find the owner and ask why it had never been published. But then he remembered where he was. These people had so much money that it became oxygen, only noticeable by a sudden absence. And few of them had the courage to face the sort of intellectual rejection that publishing your inner secrets carried.

Javier wondered how many Hemingways might be hiding out behind all the booze and complex pharmaceuticals in this place.

Four-Two and…there it was.

*Oh, crap.*

A small block carved from a white stone lit through with red threads. No bigger than two of his fingers.

A *Baiwen* seal. With a small woman's compact he just knew was filled with silk seal paste in a red so bright as to be impossible.

Talk about ancient.

Javier wondered how many millennia old that stone was. Had it originated on Earth?

He popped the cover open to quick scan the face. It was *Traditional Chinese*, the ancient'est tongue.

These people were serious.

He must have muttered something. Or stopped breathing.

Sykora was suddenly lurking over him.

"Is that it?" she asked in a near-whisper. "How does it work?"

"Give me your hand," Javier nearly giggled, pulling out the compact and twisting it open.

He dabbed the face of the *Baiwen* into the paste, just enough, and looked up expectantly.

She glowered down at him for a moment, but then curiosity apparently got the better of her. The left hand came down.

Javier grabbed it, turned it over, and pressed the chop onto the inner portion of her forearm, right where he usually got nightclub stamps after paying the cover.

"Technically, this might make you his property," Javier said.

She tried to jerk her arm back, but he was prepared and had all his weight into the grip. She barely moved.

"Bastard," she hissed.

Javier shrugged with an evil grin. Not like she didn't have it coming.

He put the stone away with all the care of a holy relic, wrapping it back up and stowing it and the paste compact into his bag.

The next document was a birth certificate in a leather satchel, two and a half centuries old, annotated with dates and subsequent births to the eighth generation, a boy who would be about thirty now. It was sealed with each addition.

Legally binding. And probably the kid's death sentence, were it found. Were he found.

Javier wondered about the people paying to destroy the evidence. At least they were willing to let the kid be.

Unless this was all some machination to have the guy killed or kidnapped later, when he was just a commoner, and no longer the true Emperor of *Changzhuo*, hiding from the people who held the planet and the government now.

Or someone had hired Navarre and expected an entirely different outcome from this.

*This is not my circus. These are not my monkeys.*

Javier took about half the papers with him. All the legal stuff. The boring identification went back into the box. He left the bank statements alone, and the bonds, and the jewelry. The kid would need them, tomorrow.

Carefully, he stowed the box back into the wall and locked it up.

"Okay," he said. "Let's go."

"You're leaving the helmet?" she asked, incredulous.

"That's right," he said. "Hopefully, she'll see it as a peace offering when she reviews the tapes and realizes how much damage we could have done."

"You're insane, Navarre," Hadiiye muttered at him.

How much of it was roleplay, he had no idea. They were long past that point.

Now they just had to get out of here alive.

PART SIX

Djamila found it educational, watching Aritza work. She could appreciate the rare moments when the man exhibited professional care and sensibilities. She just wished he would act more like a grown-up, more of the time.

She might even be able to respect him, if he did that. However long those odds might be.

He opened the boxes with ease. Never a wasted movement.

And left behind, literally, a king's ransom in the first of two boxes.

From the third box, only the stone stamp, the crimson ink, and a handful of official-looking papers.

Nothing more.

"Okay," he said. "Let's go."

"You're leaving the helmet?" she was shocked.

All that effort to find the metal, craft it. Everything. And just leave it here. What was the value, even if it wasn't a priceless antique?

"That's right," the man replied brusquely. "Hopefully,

she'll see it as a peace offering, when she reviews the tapes and realizes how much damage we could have done."

"You're insane, Navarre," Djamila growled at him.

But she couldn't really blame him.

Javier Aritza operated by his own code. Navarre had inherited the tendencies, if not the patterns.

Djamila blinked at herself, happy that Aritza was already to the door and leaving. He hadn't seen her face.

Was it possible to understand that code, and respect the man for it?

Wilhelmina Teague had suggested that just because not everyone approached life with the same focused ferocity she did, didn't mean there wasn't value in what they did.

For anybody but Aritza, Djamila was willing to understand.

He needed to get his shit together. Grow up.

Act like management.

She shook her head and followed him through the door with one last look around. But for the video of their adventures, and the faintest hint of machine oil, nobody would know they had been in here.

Out past the security trussed-up security guard, into the main hall. Just another two crew members coming off their shift, although she was trailing Aritza by about four meters.

Javier stopped cold, hands in the air.

"What are you doing now?" she hissed.

Djamila was on top of Aritza before she saw the other figure step out from a doorway.

Armed. Competent. Aimed.

*Angry.*

Farouz.

One strong hand held a pistol identical to the one on her hip. It had been centered on Aritza. Now it was aimed at her heart.

They were a simple model. Pump a great deal of energy into the target at something less than ten meters, watch them fall over.

It wasn't even a beam like a laser. More like a shotgun, impacting a target just under half a meter across at ten meters.

Nothing she could easily avoid, even with her reflexes.

"Thief in the night, Captain Navarre?" he asked in a quiet, deep voice.

"You don't know the half of it, pal," Javier growled back.

How had Farouz managed to evade the probe?

She remembered the elegant way the man had walked. How he had stalked her in the clothing closet.

Precise. Controlled. Compact.

Something like she had done. Did. Was.

*Special Operations.*

Not *Neu Berne*, but something similar. Someplace that required the efforts of a dangerous few when the applications of mass would not work.

Diamond cutter.

A killer.

"What have you done, Navarre?" Farouz continued.

"Removed a player from the board," Navarra sneered.

"Who have you assassinated, now?"

Djamila could see Farouz growing angry.

Angrier.

Short of temper.

"Nobody, Farouz," she interjected, careful not to move.

He might fire on movement. The blade was that finely balanced.

"Nobody?" the bantam sneered. "Captain Navarre and his lethal moll Hadiiye? Nobody?"

"One guard with a mild concussion," she said evenly. "The rest are papers to be destroyed."

"Papers?" Farouz asked.

She could see confusion begin in his eyes. Eyes previously a warm brown gone coldly lethal with anger.

He was not undressing her with those eyes now, appreciating her for her muscles where other men were disappointed by the lack of ponderous breasts.

No, he was measuring her for a coffin.

"Legal papers," Aritza said.

Javier's voice was less Navarre, now.

Less killer. More Science Officer.

"I do not understand."

"Birth certificates," Javier continued. "Proof of identity. Genetics registry. The works. So yeah, maybe an assassination, depending on how you want to measure it. Tomorrow, he has to become the person he's been pretending to be, all these years."

"Why?"

Djamila could measure the confusion in those eyes. She had seen her soul reflected in them before.

They were turbid.

"Because I'm more than just a mass casualty incident waiting to happen, pal," Javier growled. "Sometimes, it's possible to split a diamond with a single tap, and not a bucket of nitroglycerin."

"And you, Hadiiye?" Farouz asked. "All that to get access to the system?"

The gun never wavered from the spot exactly between her breasts. Farouz might consider Navarre dangerous, but he was taking no chances with her.

She was angry. Torn.

Not insulted at the implications. That was the cost of being in this business.

The lies that went with it.

No, this anger was for that look. That touch, standing in

the tiny closet, considering kissing this man when he asked politely, rather than all the other the men who had demanded it as some right.

The loss.

She could lie now.

The emotional break would be better.

Cleaner.

Final.

And wrong.

"That had been my mission, Farouz," she replied simply. "We went well beyond mission parameters, you and I."

"And had we gone to bed?" he snarled.

She nodded.

"That would have been of the body, Farouz," she said. "Nothing else. Nothing *more*."

He stood there, perfectly still.

Seconds passed.

She wanted to say something. Anything.

There was nothing else that needed saying.

Farouz realized that as well. Doubt disappeared from his eyes. Sadness crept in to replace it.

He nodded.

"Yes," he agreed. "You are correct."

Djamila let a small sigh escape her soul.

"So now we've got a problem, buddy," Javier said sharply. "You're not taking us in."

Djamila watched Aritza lower his hands slowly, peacefully.

"No?" Farouz asked. "And why would that be, Captain Navarre?"

"Because your boss will kill us for this," the man known as Navarre declared. "I'm not interested in that outcome."

"I'm sorry, Captain Navarre," Farouz said in a polite tone. "You no longer have a choice in the matter."

"I have lots of options, punk," Navarre rasped.

Djamila watched him take a small step to his left. Not charging directly at Farouz. Not even really threatening him.

Just moving.

She held perfectly still.

Navarre took a second step, this one closer towards Farouz.

"And you don't get to stop me," Navarre continued.

Farouz turned to point the pistol at Navarre.

Perhaps it was a threat. Perhaps a statement. Perhaps he forgot his foe.

Later, perhaps, she considered that perhaps it hadn't been an accident.

Djamila drew, aimed, and fired at a nerve speed that nobody she had ever met, and only the most expensive training robots, could match.

*The Ballerina of Death.*

Aritza had told crew members of *Storm Gauntlet* that she actively worshipped the Goddess of Destruction.

But he had no clue what made a woman like Djamila Sykora tick.

Farouz's eyes flickered back to track her faster than the pistol could follow.

It wouldn't have mattered.

No human could have reversed course and gotten off a shot.

Even Farouz only came close.

This model of pistol was nearly silent, save for the faintest pop in the air, mostly static electricity bleeding off the target as every nerve overloaded and everything inside went to white noise.

It didn't even have the physical kick of a small chuck of lead slamming into someone at the speed of sound. Nothing to knock a man back. Nothing to indicate success.

Farouz just crumpled silently to the ground.

Only his pistol made a sound, clattering loudly as it tumbled into a corner from nerveless hands.

Djamila ranted in several languages in her head.

Nothing showed on the outside.

*Neu Berne.*

Navarre turned a cold eye on her.

No, not Navarre.

Aritza.

"I will say this exactly once," he said in a quiet voice. "If asked later, I will deny everything. Do we need to kidnap this man and take him with us?"

Djamila stared daggers at the man. Wished she could strangle him with her bare hands.

He had seen weakness. Identified it. Could exploit it later.

And yet…

He was offering to do something *for* her, rather than to her.

Farouz might never forgive her. Either way. And the chances of them ever meeting again were pitifully low, unless one sought out the other.

And she did not dare.

For that way lay weakness. Fallible flesh.

Wilhelmina Teague appeared in her vision for a split second. Perhaps her memory.

"No, Djamila," Dr. Teague replied calmly. "We call that humanity."

Djamila growled. Mostly under her breath.

Took a deep breath. Held it.

Let it go.

"No," she finally said, after an eternal heartbeat. "He will understand."

She grabbed the tiny man and lifted him carefully, almost lovingly.

The door to the security room was closed. Locked.

"Open it," she commanded Aritza, trailing in her wake.

He did and stepped quickly aside as she entered.

Farouz would be out for a while. Long enough.

They could still make their escape.

Most of her would.

A small part of her soul, she knew she would leave on this deck.

PART SEVEN

THE LAND LEVIATHAN had not changed, except to roll perhaps a thousand miles forward in time and space.

Javier found the desert air dry and nasty. It fit his mood.

Two months had passed. Four since he had first landed on the big iron whale. Sokolov and *Storm Gauntlet* had been up to minor jobs, but nothing particularly profitable.

Keeping the lights on and the crew in socks and cream.

It was the same limo flying them in, with the same blemish in the right armrest. Zakhar had napped again.

They landed on the same last platform and disembarked to the same hard man in the nice suit. The two killers were different, but they were the same.

Javier wore the same Navarre outfit from before. Boots, britches, doublet, headband.

The only difference was the satchel he held in one hand. An old, leather and canvas job he had found in *Storm Gauntlet*'s Lost and Found, left over from some Barrister that had been through.

And the belt with the sword and the pulse pistol.

Unlike last time, it was charged.

The hard man held out a hand, expecting Javier to hand over his weapons.

"No," Navarre snarled back.

The man blinked, reconsidered, and survived the day.

Javier paid more attention as he walked. They were aboard the fourth car, having crossed from each on a catwalk to the next.

She was there. Like before.

Stewart Lace. Banker to pirates. Fixer for people needing things fixed.

Still well dressed. Still proper. Still fadingly beautiful.

Tea. Cheese and garlic scones. Antipasti plate.

Civilized.

Javier sat between her and Captain Sokolov.

Pinkies were out.

Javier decided he had played enough. He sat down his tea mug and saucer and reached for the satchel. Inside, a smaller leather carryall that Kianoush had whipped up to transport the priceless artifacts.

That came out. Madame Lace quickly rested her tea in order to take the prize from him.

She shared a secret smile with him as their fingers touched.

"My backer was surprised at the outcome, Captain Navarre," she purred.

"That's because you work for a moron," Javier barked back at her.

It had taken nearly a month to get Navarre to finally shut up. This woman had the potential to mess with his *wa*.

Unacceptable.

"Were you expecting a marine assault?" he sneered. "Perhaps a full ambush with pulse cannons and ship-killing missiles? Abraam Tamaz?"

"I believe that was more in keeping with their expectations, yes," she said, a trifle on defense.

Obviously, she hadn't been immune to that line of logic, either.

Fool.

"Fine," Javier said diplomatically. "Understand that this will be the last job for that patron. Ever. Next time, tell them to hire a psychopath."

"Instead of a professional?" she teased.

"You wanted a job done, Lace," Sokolov said. "If you wanted more, the price would have probably been too high, even for them."

"I see," she replied, opening the case.

Nothing had changed. Chop in a nice little felt bag. Cerise inker. Eight pieces of paper rolled up carefully.

She looked up, fixed Javier with a hard eye.

"Ask now, Madame Lace," Javier growled. "This topic is off-limits tomorrow."

"How did you manage everything?" she finally inquired. "I had been told the job would have been impossible without significant casualties. And yet you managed."

"No," Javier went cold. "Trade secrets. End of discussion."

"I can appreciate that," Lace said with a discreet nod.

She turned and pulled a small messenger bag of her own out from behind a pillow.

In the blink of an eye, Javier had nearly shot her. Well, Navarre had.

Close enough.

She opened the small bag with a great deal more care than she had grabbed for it. Maybe she realized how close she had been to dying, just now.

Kianoush's bag went in. Two small envelopes came out.

The first went to Zakhar.

"Captain Sokolov," she nodded gravely. "Receipt of a payment wired into your account, as contracted. With a small bonus."

Zakhar accepted in utter silence.

"Captain Navarre," Stewart Lace said in a most reserved voice. "This second envelope was delivered to me by way of several layers of intermediaries. It has not been opened, but it has been scanned for danger. We have not read the message, but are confident that it is safe."

Javier grunted.

Even from here, he could smell the perfume she had infused into the paper. It was better than a signature.

The writing on the front was calligraphic, but legible. Perfect. Like she was.

*E. Navarre.*

Another clue. As if he needed one.

Javier took it from the woman's hand and stuffed it into his unbuttoned doublet.

There was no way in hell he was opening it here.

"Thank you," he said.

Nothing more.

Nothing needed.

Javier took her by surprise by rising.

"Madame Lace," he bowed formally. "Perhaps we will meet again. In less uncertain circumstances."

She rose and took his hand. Firm. Strong.

Ever so slightly damp.

Flop sweat was a bitch.

And then he left, leaving Sokolov to trail in his wake. Hard man and the two killers waited outside the room, escorted them silently back to the VTOL, remained behind when they took off.

Zakhar started to say something, but thought better of it. He closed his eyes and leaned back instead.

It was as much privacy as Javier would get, at least until he got back to the ship.

The envelope was lavender paper. The ink was probably real vermillion, the expensive kind and not just the product of a good chemistry lab. She was like that.

The seal was wax, melted and pressed with a signet ring, leaving a unique imprint of *Shangdu.*

The paper was a heavy, handmade stock randomly multi-colored from the source material.

Her handwriting was simply exquisite.

*E,*

*It is obvious that you can get into places you were never intended. And do so with care and style, not damaging things without a purpose. Thank you. Farouz has recovered from his anger, as well.*

*I am keeping the helmet. As you said, a peace offering. And it fits marvelously.*

*It is my wish that you not necessarily be a stranger, and we not be enemies. Perhaps I might even be able to put your unique skills to occasional use. There is great potential.*

*B*

*p.s. And please enjoy the enclosed and think of me occasionally.*

JAVIER REACHED BACK into the envelope. There was a smaller envelope inside, like a matryoska doll. And inside that envelope was a picture printed on paper, like an antique, ten centimeters by twenty.

The face was obscured, shadowed, by masterful use of lighting and the way the Helm of Athena's cheek pieces came down. Only her smile was clear.

And she had pulled her long, black hair down and around her, just enough to make the picture cheesecake and not porn, but it was obvious that she wasn't wearing anything but the helmet as she kneeled on what had been his bed.

The picture hanging from the wall in the background gave that away.

She was still utterly exquisite, but you had to have seen the *Khatum of Altai* that way previously, completely nude, to recognize her now.

The galaxy's most beautiful black widow spider. Possibly the deadliest, as well.

Javier found himself as frightened of seeing her again as he was aroused at the prospect.

If he walked back into her web, would he ever escape? Did he want to?

Javier smiled and laughed under his breath.

"What did she say?" Zakhar asked, never opening his eyes.

"You knew?" Javier replied.

"I've read your report," Sokolov said. "And I know you well enough to read between the lines. Two plus two still equals four when you're around."

Javier laughed a second time.

"So maybe everything will turn out okay, after all," Javier said.

"I could have told you that, Mr. Science Officer," Sokolov said. "You just never want to listen."

Javier had to give the man that. They shared that much heritage.

Dancing with a black widow had gotten him so much closer to paying off his debt to the man.

Maybe he needed spin his own webs.

After all, he still had to kill Sykora, one of these days.

READ MORE!

Be sure to pick up the other books in The Science Officer series!

*The Science Officer*
*The Mind Field*
*The Gilded Cage*
*The Pleasure Dome*
*The Doomsday Vault*
*The Last Flagship*
*The Hammerfield Gambit*
*The Hammerfield Payoff*

You can get volumes 1-4 collected together in
*The Science Officer Omnibus 1*

Volumes 5-8 are collected together in
*The Science Officer Omnibus 2*

# ABOUT THE AUTHOR

Blaze Ward writes science fiction in the Alexandria Station universe (Jessica Keller, The Science Officer, The Story Road, etc.) as well as several other science fiction universes, such as Star Dragon, the Dominion, and more. He also writes odd bits of high fantasy with swords and orcs. In addition, he is the Editor and Publisher of *Boundary Shock Quarterly Magazine.* You can find out more at his website www.blazeward.com, as well as Facebook, Goodreads, and other places.

Blaze's works are available as ebooks, paper, and audio, and can be found at a variety of online vendors. His newsletter comes out regularly, and you can also follow his blog on his website. He really enjoys interacting with fans, and looks forward to any and all questions—even ones about his books!

### Reviews

It's true. Reviews help me sell more books. If you've enjoyed this story, please consider leaving a review of it on your favorite site.

### Never miss a release!
If you'd like to be notified of new releases, sign up for my newsletter.

I will never spam you or use your email for nefarious purposes. You can also unsubscribe at any time.

http://www.blazeward.com/newsletter/

**Connect with Blaze!**

Web: www.blazeward.com
Boundary Shock Quarterly (BSQ):
https://www.boundaryshockquarterly.com/

# ABOUT KNOTTED ROAD PRESS

Knotted Road Press fiction specializes in dynamic writing set in mysterious, exotic locations.

Knotted Road Press non-fiction publishes autobiographies, business books, cookbooks, and how-to books with unique voices.

Knotted Road Press creates DRM-free ebooks as well as high-quality print books for readers around the world.

With authors in a variety of genres including literary, poetry, mystery, fantasy, and science fiction, Knotted Road Press has something for everyone.

Knotted Road Press<br>www.KnottedRoadPress.com

www.ingramcontent.com/pod-product-compliance
Lightning Source LLC
Chambersburg PA
CBHW071825190726
48292CB00005B/1607